P9-CQC-253

"Oh, Caleb." She wrapped her arms around him and he clung to her, his head resting against hers, warm hands pressed against her back.

She smoothed her palms up and down his spine, a comforting gesture, though she couldn't help but be aware of the muscles beneath her touch. Caleb was her friend, but he wanted her. And she wanted him.

She tilted her head to look at him, and as if in response, he leaned in to kiss her. Something broke in her at that moment, and she closed her eyes and gave herself up to that kiss, letting go of everything she had been holding back so long.

He switched from kissing her mouth to trailing his lips along her jaw, all the way to her ear. "Do you want me to stop?" he asked.

"No." She pulled him against her more tightly.

"We agreed this was wrong."

"Do you really believe that?" she asked.

PAM

SECRETS OF SILVERPEAK MINE

Cindi Myers

—

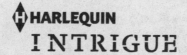

HARLEQUIN
INTRIGUE

If you purchased this book without a cover you should be aware
that this book is stolen property. It was reported as "unsold and
destroyed" to the publisher, and neither the author nor the
publisher has received any payment for this "stripped book."

For Dawn

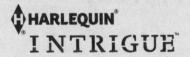

ISBN-13: 978-1-335-59056-5

Secrets of Silverpeak Mine

Copyright © 2023 by Cynthia Myers

All rights reserved. No part of this book may be used or reproduced in
any manner whatsoever without written permission except in the case of
brief quotations embodied in critical articles and reviews.

This is a work of fiction. Names, characters, places and incidents
are either the product of the author's imagination or are used fictitiously.
Any resemblance to actual persons, living or dead, businesses,
companies, events or locales is entirely coincidental.

For questions and comments about the quality of this book,
please contact us at CustomerService@Harlequin.com.

Harlequin Enterprises ULC
22 Adelaide St. West, 41st Floor
Toronto, Ontario M5H 4E3, Canada
www.Harlequin.com

Printed in U.S.A.

Recycling programs
for this product may
not exist in your area.

Cindi Myers is the author of more than seventy-five novels. When she's not plotting new romance story lines, she enjoys skiing, gardening, cooking, crafting and daydreaming. A lover of small-town life, she lives with her husband and two spoiled dogs in the Colorado mountains.

Books by Cindi Myers

Harlequin Intrigue

Eagle Mountain: Critical Response

Eagle Mountain Search and Rescue

Eagle Mountain: Search for Suspects

The Ranger Brigade: Rocky Mountain Manhunt

Visit the Author Profile page at Harlequin.com.

CAST OF CHARACTERS

Danielle Priest—Newly pregnant and abandoned by her lover, Danielle comes to Eagle Mountain to regroup and to help discover the identity of the woman whose skeleton was found at the bottom of a mine shaft.

Caleb Garrison—Search and rescue rookie Caleb retrieved the skeleton from the mine shaft, worried that it might belong to his estranged wife, Nora. He hopes Danielle will provide the answers he's been looking for about what happened to Nora after she left him.

Nora Garrison—The blonde beauty charmed and manipulated Caleb into marrying her, then ran off with his new truck and most of his money. He hasn't seen her in almost two years, though he hired a private detective to look for her.

Jane Doe—No one seems to know the identity of the young woman whose skeleton was found in the mine or how she ended up in such a remote location. Danielle's reconstruction of her face only raises more questions.

Carissa Miller—Danielle's neighbor in Eagle Mountain is expecting a baby, too. But Danielle is worried about her new friend, whose husband is overbearing and overprotective.

Joey Miller—Carissa's overprotective husband bothers Danielle, but Carissa is devoted to him.

Chapter One

"You volunteered for this."

Caleb Garrison muttered this reminder as he clung to the curved rock wall of a mine air shaft. He tried not to think of what awaited him below. The climb wasn't difficult. The shaft was narrow but not dangerously so. Routine stuff, really. He didn't have to hurry, and he had plenty of support up at ground level. But still, a shiver rippled up his spine and he forced himself not to look down. He wasn't ready yet to see what was down there.

"I need someone who isn't claustrophobic to rappel into the air shaft at Silverpeak Mine," Eagle Mountain Search and Rescue Captain Sheri Stevens had announced when the volunteers assembled for what was billed as a non-emergency callout.

"I can do that," Caleb said before anyone else had a chance. As a rookie, he was trying to get as many hours in as he could. He wanted to prove he had what it took for physically and mentally demanding rescue work.

Sheri looked him in the eye, her expression daunting. "You'd be going down there to retrieve human remains," she said. "Are you okay with that?"

Caleb swallowed. This was part of the job too, wasn't it? His early training had made that clear. Despite the team's best efforts, not everyone survived the kind of trouble people could get into in this rough country. "I can do it," he said, though he wasn't 100 percent sure about that.

"From what we can tell, you'll be bringing up bones." Rayford County Sheriff's Deputy Dwight Prentice, who had been standing alongside Sheri, said. "Whoever this is looks to have been down there a long time."

"So we're talking more of a skeleton than a body?" Caleb asked. That didn't sound so bad.

"Yeah," Dwight said. "But you need to be careful. Take a lot of pictures before you touch anything, and make sure you bring up everything—the bones and anything near them. Anything you find could be evidence."

"Evidence of what?" Caleb asked.

Dwight shrugged. "Of who this person was and how they died."

"You don't think this guy—or girl—was murdered, do you?" Caleb asked.

"We won't know until we get a closer look." Dwight clapped him on the shoulder. "Which is where you come in."

"How's it going?" Sheri called down from above. She leaned over the shaft and looked down on him, blotting out part of the circle of blue sky.

"Great," he called. "I'm almost down." He made a point of picking up the pace of his descent. Better to get this over with, so they could all go home. He braced his feet against the rough rock walls and carefully lowered himself to the bottom of the shaft, some thirty feet below the surface. He was careful to keep close to the wall as he landed, not wanting to step on any of the bones scattered on the gravel at his feet. Avoiding tangling in the ropes, he steeled himself and turned to face the scene.

The bones were in a heap just across from him, the afternoon sun overhead spotlighting the pile, the skull on top, the empty eye sockets gazing up at the sky. They had been down here a long time, he guessed, with no skin or hair clinging to them, but plenty of fine reddish dust. There was no smell of decay—just dust and rock. In the pile he could make out the rib cage, and the long bones of the arms and legs, the pelvis and lots of small unidentifiable pieces. Maybe it wasn't even a real skeleton, but a discarded Halloween decoration? Even as the thought entered his mind, he discarded it. The bones looked real, all right. How had they ended up here?

"Before you touch anything, we need lots of pictures, in situ." This came from a male voice. Caleb looked up to see Dwight looking down on him.

"I remember," Caleb said. He and Sheri and the other SAR members who showed up to provide support had waited almost an hour while Dwight and the sheriff and the medical examiner, Butch Collins, discussed whether or not to try to get a forensics team into the shaft. A portly man with a tonsure of gray hair, Butch was dressed in faded green cords, a flannel shirt worn thin at the elbows and a fishing vest, the pockets stuffed with tackle. Caleb wondered if the retired doctor had been summoned mid-cast, though he had betrayed no annoyance at being called to this remote location on a Saturday afternoon.

The authorities had finally decided to let Caleb go by himself, partly because no one else wanted to descend into that narrow shaft on the end of a rope, and because looking down into the air shaft, there didn't appear to be much that Caleb could disturb.

Caleb slipped his cell phone from the pocket of his pants and focused the camera lens on the scene. Just beyond the bones he could see a pile of rubble—a collapsed tunnel from the long-defunct Silverpeak Mine. Did these bones belong to a miner who had been trapped by the tunnel collapse? Had he perished here, in sight of freedom, but unable to climb out?

Caleb shuddered and pushed the thought away. He snapped off half a dozen shots from different angles, then reached for the plastic bag clipped to his harness. He was supposed to gather all the bones and bring them up in this.

"Do you see any signs of foul play?" Dwight called down.

Caleb looked to the bones again. "There's not an ax sticking out of the skull, or a knife between the ribs, if that's what you mean," he said. Maybe that was crass, but black humor was par for the course in a situation like this, wasn't it?

"Be sure you bring up any clothing and anything else near the body," Dwight called down.

"There isn't any clothing," Caleb said. That absence hadn't struck him when he had been looking down from above, but now that he was with the bones, it seemed odd that they were so, well, naked. Miners—if this was a miner—wore thick canvas pants and heavy hobnailed boots. Mines were damp and cold even in summer, so the miners also wore layers to keep warm—woolen long underwear and multiple shirts. Though textiles disintegrated with time, some fragments ought to remain. Items like the boots and iron buckles and leather straps could last for centuries.

"No clothing?" Dwight asked. "Are you sure?"

Caleb took a step closer and bent toward the bones. "There's nothing," he said. "Not even a scrap of fabric or leather or anything."

"Huh," came the single syllable from overhead. A long pause, then, "Is there anything that might identify the person those bones belong to?"

Caleb scanned the area carefully. He taught college-level history in his day job, and had a particular interest in the mining heritage of the area. He had been in a few historic mines, and most of them were littered with relics of their heyday—broken iron picks, bits of shovels and miner's candles with the sharp ends of the metal holders still stuck into the walls of the mines, where their flickering flames had provided the only light to work by. Belt buckles, lunch pails, old bottles, bits of harness, broken dishes—every mine was a treasure trove of artifacts. He pulled a flashlight from his pocket and directed its beam along the edges of the wall in the circular space. Except for the bones and a few dried leaves, the place looked swept clean. "There's nothing here," he said. "Nothing but the bones."

"Do they look like they've been there a long time?" Dwight asked.

"A long time," Caleb said. "They're really, um, clean." He touched the center of an arm bone—the ulna, he thought—with one gloved finger. Dust smudged at his touch, but the bone's surface was smooth, almost polished.

"Bring up everything," Dwight said. "Anything at all that you find."

"Right." Caleb opened the bag and bent to gather up the bones. He decided the best approach was to sort of sweep everything into the bag, keeping the stack together and disturbing the bones as little as possible. His earlier nervousness was replaced by curiosity. Whose bones were these? And what were they doing at the bottom of a mine air shaft in the remote mountains of southwest Colorado?

Twenty minutes later he had fastened the bag to a rope and sent it up the air shaft. He made a last sweep of the area and verified there was nothing left for him to retrieve, then grabbed hold of the rope he had descended on and started the climb up.

He emerged to find Dwight and Butch bent over the open plastic bag, staring at the jumbled bones. "You got good photos?" Dwight asked.

Caleb nodded and handed his phone to the deputy. Dwight scrolled though the images on the screen and nodded. "Send them to me," he said, and rattled off a number. "As soon as you get back in cell service."

"Will do," Caleb said, and entered the number into his phone. Sheri moved in to help him unclip from the ropes, and fellow SAR volunteer Tony Meisner accepted Caleb's helmet and harness. "Have you ever had to retrieve a skeleton before?" Caleb asked. Tony had been with Eagle Mountain Search and Rescue over twenty years, longer than any other volunteer.

Tony shook his head. "This is definitely a first."

"Who called this in?" Caleb asked.

"The call came from the man who just purchased this mining claim," Sheri said, joining them. A tall, slender woman with short blond hair, she had the respect of the volunteers who served under her, and was acknowledged to be one of their best climbers. Though Caleb had been climbing as a pastime for a while, he had learned a lot under Sheri's tutelage. "He said he was getting ready to put an iron grate over the air shaft. He was worried about an animal falling in and getting trapped. When he looked into the shaft, he thought at first the bones belonged to an animal. Then he saw the skull and decided he had better call the sheriff." She shrugged. "When they saw where the bones were, they called us to go after him."

Tony glanced toward the air shaft. "I wonder how he died."

"The mine tunnel leading to the air shaft has collapsed," Caleb said. "Maybe he was trapped. He couldn't climb out, or he tried to climb out and fell?"

"Seems like the other miners would have known he was in there," Tony said.

"There might not have been other miners," Caleb said. "A lot of these smaller claims were one-man operations. And a lot of the early miners were single men who came here, often from other countries, to seek their fortune. If he had family, they might not have known where to look for him."

"It's a bit of a historical mystery, then." Tony looked up as the medical examiner approached. "What do you think, Doc?" he asked.

"I'll have to take a closer look when I get the bones to the morgue," Butch said. "It's odd that there was no clothing with the body." He glanced over at the air shaft. "Not to be macabre, but this would make a good dump site."

Caleb stared. "But those bones must have been down there a really long time," he said. "I mean, I'm no expert, but for them to be that clean, that would take years, right?"

"I understand you're up on your local history," Butch said. "You work with the local historical society, right?"

"I volunteer to help with their archives," Caleb said. "And I teach history at Colorado State."

"Any missing persons cases way back that you've heard of?" Butch asked.

"Nothing like that." Caleb shrugged. "But I haven't really looked into historical crimes. My focus is on early mining. And I can tell you, lots of accidents happened. It was dangerous work under some pretty harsh conditions, without modern safety equipment."

"That's probably what this is," Butch said. "But I have to eliminate all the other more grisly possibilities." He offered his hand. "Thanks for your help today." He shook Caleb and Tony's hands, then ambled away. Dwight followed, carrying the plastic bag of bones, a prosaic ending for a most unusual callout.

"Good job today," Sheri said, turning her attention to Caleb once more. "Even though the skeleton was old, that had to be unnerving, being down there with it in such close quarters."

"It was at first," Caleb said. "But when I focused on thinking about them from the perspective of a historian, it helped. Like Tony said, it's a bit of a historical mystery. I'm going to check the historical society archives and see if I can find out more about the Silverpeak Mine. Who knows? Maybe I'll learn the name of the poor guy."

"Let us know if you do." Sheri checked her watch. "Let's get the gear loaded and wrap this up. I want to get cleaned up in time for the dance tonight."

"You mean the fundraiser for Mickey Dexter?" Tony asked. "Kelsey and I will be there." He turned to Caleb. "Are you going? I've heard the band before and they're really good."

Caleb shook his head. "I'm not much of a dancer."

"You don't have to dance," Sheri said. "There will be food and a silent auction. And it's for a good cause. Mickey's a really great guy and his friends are raising money to help with his medical bills."

"Stage four cancer," Tony said. "But Mickey's a real fighter. If anyone can make it, he can."

"I'll be sure to contribute," Caleb said. "But

I have papers I need to be grading." It was a convenient excuse for a teacher, right?

"There will always be papers to grade," Sheri said. He had forgotten that she taught at Eagle Mountain High School. "You should come. It will be a great way for you to meet more people."

"I'll think about it." But Caleb didn't want to meet more people. He already had plenty of friends. And if by *people* Sheri meant *women*, he didn't need to meet any of them, either. It wasn't as if he had anything to offer a woman, other than news that he already had a wife he hadn't laid eyes on in almost two years. And if he never saw her again, he wouldn't be the least bit sorry.

Chapter Two

"If you would listen to reason, you wouldn't have to do this." Assistant District Attorney Richard Ernst watched Danielle Priest as she packed the items from her desk in Denver's crime lab into a cardboard box. He stood with his arms folded, the muscles of his biceps and shoulders straining the fabric of his shirt. Richard was proud of those muscles. He spent a lot of time in the gym sculpting them and he had his shirts specially tailored to show them to advantage.

Danielle bit the inside of her cheek and shoved another reference book into the box, next to the makeup bag, coffee mug and miscellaneous flotsam and jetsam from the desk drawers. There wasn't much to take with her. The models she had crafted with such care belonged to the lab, and she had no desire to keep the framed photos of her with her colleagues, most of them featuring Richard. In one, he stood next to her, one arm around her shoulder, smiling in a way she had thought at the time was affectionate, but now she only saw as smug.

If she let herself open her mouth now, she would scream at him, and then she would cry, and then everyone in this part of the City and County of Denver offices would overhear and her departure from the job she loved and did well would be even more undignified.

She leaned over to yank open the last drawer and Richard moved in to block her. He leaned close, his breath stirring her hair where it curled around her left ear. "I'm not only thinking about me," he said, his voice low. Seductive. At least she had thought of it that way once. "This decision of yours is going to wreak havoc on your career."

She pulled at the drawer, hitting him sharply in the shin. He jumped back, face mottled red now. Her determination to not talk to him failed and she glared at him. "You're the one who decided you didn't want this baby." She rested one arm on her abdomen. At twelve weeks her pregnancy wasn't advanced enough for most people to notice, but she knew the baby was there. The baby he had called a *mistake* and *not my problem*.

He looked around. "Keep your voice down," he hissed.

She lowered her voice. Not out of consideration for him, but for her own protection. She wasn't ready for all their coworkers to know what a fool she had been. "You don't have to worry," she said. "After all, you're getting what you want. I'm getting out of your life, and I'm taking my baby with me."

She glanced in the drawer, saw nothing she needed in there and slammed it shut hard enough that a stack of files in her inbox wobbled precariously. Not her problem now. She started to move around the desk and Richard grabbed her arm. "Dani," he said, his voice tender. Coaxing. Oh, how she would have melted at that tone even a few weeks ago. Back when she thought of him as a lover and not a snake. "I never wanted you out of my life. I love you and I want us to be together."

"Don't you think your *fiancée* might object to that?" She jerked her arm away and moved to put the desk between them.

He assumed a hurt expression. "Marrying Jenna is just a career move, you understand that, don't you? You and I don't have to stop seeing each other. I know how to be discreet."

So discreet she had had no idea he even knew Jenna Anderson, much less had been dating her for six months. Danielle wasn't naive enough to believe he really loved Jenna, any more than he had loved her. The only person Richard loved was himself. But Jenna was the mayor's daughter, and marrying her fit in perfectly with Richard's aspirations to move up in local politics and eventually the state and national political scene. Jenna would be a big asset to him, while Danielle would only be a liability.

She forced herself to look him in the eye, and modulated her voice to match his coaxing tone. "So all I have to do in order for us to be together is give up this baby and keep our relationship a secret, is that it?"

Something like relief filled his eyes and his smile became genuine. "Yes, that's it!"

"That's asking a lot, Richard."

"I know." He leaned across and rubbed her arm. "But I promise I'll make it up to you. We'll take a trip together soon. Maybe Fiji? They have amazing beaches there and you look so hot in a bikini."

He was lucky she had already packed away the silver letter opener she had received as an award from a local business women's group. It would have been so tempting to stab him with it at that moment. Instead, she straightened. "I have another idea," she said. "I could stay here in this job and keep the baby. Go on with my life like before."

He blanched. "What would you tell people about the baby?" he asked.

"The truth," she said. "After all, don't they say honesty is the best policy?"

His expression hardened. "I'll deny every word of it," he said.

"DNA doesn't lie, Richard. I believe you've said that before. In court."

He planted his fists on the desk and leaned toward her. "You're trying to get money out of me, aren't you?" he asked. "You think you can blackmail me. But it won't work. If you tell anyone that child is mine, I'll tell them all about the months you spent in that psychiatric hospital back East. I'll tell them how unstable you are."

She tried to hide the fear, but she knew the moment Richard recognized it. An icy chill shuddered through her, and he no doubt saw that, too. "I'll ask for custody of the child," he said. "And I'll get it, too. No judge would agree that someone with your mental health history is fit to be a mother."

She gripped the back of the desk chair. "You need to leave now, Richard," she said.

"I will," he said. "But remember what I said. I hold all the cards here, Danielle. If I don't co-operate, you've got nothing."

She waited until he was gone before she sank into the chair, her legs no longer willing to support her, her stomach heaving. She closed her eyes and pressed her forehead to the desk, fighting the nausea and fear. Why did she let him get to her like this? Why wasn't she strong enough to stand up to him?

She focused on breathing deeply. In and out, counting to herself, willing herself to calm. After a while she was able to lift her head again. She couldn't stand up to Richard because she knew people would believe him when he claimed she was unstable. She had already attracted enough negative attention by breaking down in tears—on camera—in the middle of a press conference. Now most of her colleagues and probably all of the public thought she was unbalanced or just weird. Not the type of person who could be trusted to handle a demanding and delicate job. After all, the families of victims depended on her to do a good job of reconstructing the images of their loved ones so that they could be identified and the people who had harmed them brought to justice.

Her gaze lit on another framed photo—this one of her alone. Well, her and five mannequin heads arranged on a table in front of her. Except these weren't mannequin heads. They were the reconstructed faces of the five women whose bodies had been found in the basement of a house in the foothills west of Denver. Five girls, really, since the oldest had been only fifteen. Danielle had given those girls their identities again. She had given their families the closure of knowing what had happened to their daughters, no matter how tragic the circumstances. And she had helped to convict the evil man who had killed them. The case had been one of her proudest moments, and her most heartbreaking.

And in the midst of all of that incredible strain, she had learned she was pregnant. She had been stunned. Then terrified. Then overjoyed. She had naively expected Richard to share her feelings. She knew about his political aspirations. She even supported them. Being a family man would be a good thing, wouldn't it?

So when he had informed her that he couldn't possibly be a father and she would have to *do something* about the baby, she had been stunned. The next day she had seen the announcement in the paper about his engagement to Jenna Anderson. It had taken every ounce of will she possessed not to let the old blackness and despair wash over her. Somehow she had found the strength to say no. But she also knew herself well enough to know she couldn't stay here, with his office just one floor above.

She had turned in her resignation that morning, telling her boss she had to leave due to a family emergency. She rubbed her hand back and forth across her abdomen. It wasn't a lie. The child growing in her was her family now. She had to do what was best to protect herself and her child. Some women would have been strong enough to stay and fight Richard, but she wasn't one of them.

She never should have told Richard about her breakdown. That was seven years ago, before she came to this job. She was working in her very first position as a forensic anthropologist at the time, on a case involving five dead children. The horror of that case had broken her, literally, and she had sought in-patient treatment to heal. She had tried to change careers but her old mentor had found her and persuaded her that she had a real gift for facial reconstruction. She could make a difference to so many families by identifying their loved ones and helping law enforcement to put away killers.

So she had come to Denver and started over. And for seven years, she had done well. She had worked with local law enforcement to give faces to men and women and children who were the victims of crimes that might have gone unprosecuted if not for her. She had given closure to families who had suffered years of not knowing what had happened to their loved ones. She had done good work.

But she had been lonely. And when the handsome assistant district attorney had approached her with his easy smile and warm manner, she had been drawn to him. He had wooed her with fancy gifts and lavish words of love and she had soaked it all in like a dry lake bed blessed with rain. She hadn't seen how manipulative he was, how every decision he made was for his own benefit, not hers. Now she had to do what was best for her. For her and her baby.

She stood and shoved a plastic container of nuts and a computer mouse pad with a picture of her cat, Mrs. Marmalade, into the box. She fit the lid to the box and hefted it. Not much weight for five years of her life.

She made her way to her car without running into anyone else, shoved the box in the back, then sat in the driver's seat, keys in hand, shaking too hard to trust herself to drive. Her doctor and her therapist had both advised leaving her job as the healthiest thing she could do. Then why did the parting make her feel worse? As if she was, indeed, running away.

She gasped as her phone rang, the strains of Vivaldi seeming overloud in the still parking garage. She relaxed her shoulders a little as she read the name on the screen and answered. "Butch," she said. "How are you?" She pictured Butch Collins as he had looked in the Christmas card he had sent, which featured a photo of him on some sun-sparkled river with a backdrop of mountains, a large rainbow trout cradled lovingly in his thick-fingered hands.

"I'm good," he said. "But I need a favor from you."

"Anything." She sat up straighter. She and Butch had been friends since she had worked under him as a lowly student years ago. He had been there for her during her breakdown, and he had given her a glowing reference that had helped her get this job in Denver. They had kept in touch over the years, and he had been one of the few people to reach out to her after that disastrous press conference last week. She hadn't told him the sordid details that had led to her breakdown, and he hadn't asked. She had texted him this morning to tell him she was leaving her job, giving as the reason only that she *needed a break*.

"Could you come to Eagle Mountain?" he asked. "For a few weeks, probably. We've got a case here—some remains we can't identify. I think you could help us out. We've got a grant to pay you, and you can stay in the apartment over my garage. Private entrance and I won't be all up in your business."

She opened her mouth to refuse. The last thing she wanted right now was to work. "We could really use your help," Butch said, probably sensing her hesitation. "And you would love it here. It's so beautiful. Very peaceful."

She had never been to Eagle Mountain, but Butch talked about it the way some people talked about their lovers. He described the wild-flower-dotted meadows and snow-capped peaks, the icy streams and clear air and the good people who lived there. It sounded too good to be true, and a little too remote for her comfort. After all, it was six hours from Denver.

Six hours from Richard. Six hours from everyone who knew her and knew the gossip about her. "If you really think I can help," she said, doubt coloring every word.

"I know you can," Butch said. "Please say you'll come. We really need you."

Not half as much as she needed the distraction. "All right," she said. They discussed a few more details, and by the time she ended the call she felt calm enough to start the car and pull out of the garage. Richard would no doubt accuse her of running even farther away—across the state to a remote backwater. She doubted she was going to change much of anything by reconstructing the remains Butch had in his care, but maybe getting to work on something new, something low-risk, would help her. Eagle Mountain sounded like a good place to heal, and that was what she needed most of all.

Chapter Three

Caleb was hunched over the computer at his desk in his home, reading a paper about the Missouri Compromise written by one of his freshmen students, when his text message alert sounded. When he saw Sheri's name on the screen, his heart beat a little faster, anticipating a search and rescue callout. What would it be this time—an automobile wreck, an injured hiker or even a rafting accident? He had been unsure about search and rescue when a climbing friend had invited him to join the group, but in the last few months he had discovered the satisfaction—and excitement—of rallying to help someone in a dire situation. Even the retrieval of those bones from the mine had been a test of his nerve and interesting from a historical perspective.

He scrolled to the message.

Press conference at sheriff's department 1:00 p.m. re: bones found in mine. Thought you might want to attend.

Caleb frowned. Sheriff Travis Walker was known for keeping quiet about the department's business. In the nine months since Caleb had relocated to Eagle Mountain, he didn't think Travis had held a single press conference. What about those old bones had prompted this?

He checked his watch. It was 12:30 p.m. He had just enough time to gather his things and head over to the sheriff's department.

When he got there, he found Sheri, Tony and several other members of Search and Rescue waiting. "What's up?" Caleb asked, squeezing in between Sheri and fellow SAR volunteer Ryan Welch.

Sheri shook her head. "No idea. Jake texted me to let me know about the press conference right before I sent the word to the rest of the team."

Jake Gwynn was a Search and Rescue volunteer, and also a sheriff's deputy. "Maybe the medical examiner found evidence of a crime," Ryan said.

"Any unsolved murders in the historical archives?" Tony asked.

"I don't think so," Caleb said. He had only

had time to do a superficial search for missing miners, but he hadn't come up with anything so far.

A murmur at the front of the crowded conference room drew their attention. Caleb looked up to see the sheriff, Sergeant Gage Walker, Travis's brother, and Butch Collins enter the room. The two Walker brothers, both tall and good-looking, with dark hair and eyes, made a sharp contrast with the portly balding medical examiner. Travis waited until the gathering was silent before he spoke. "Three days ago, Search and Rescue volunteers helped in the recovery of skeletal human remains from an air shaft at the Silverpeak Mine up on Columbine Mountain," Travis said. "The medical examiner has determined that the skeleton is that of a female, aged twenty-five to forty-five, approximately five feet six inches tall. We're asking the public to help us identify this woman, who had no clothing or other identifying items with her."

A new murmur rose from the crowd. Caleb and Sheri exchanged surprised looks. *Eagle Mountain Examiner* reporter Tammy Patterson, stationed at the front of the room, asked, "How did the woman die? What was she doing in that old mine?"

Travis looked over his shoulder to Butch, who stepped to the microphone. "There are signs of head trauma, but that may have happened when the body was dropped or thrown into the air shaft."

"You don't think she died at the mine?" someone else asked.

"No," Butch said.

"When did she die?" Tammy asked. "Was she a miner's wife? Or someone else associated with the mines?"

Travis again looked to Butch, who cleared his throat and leaned toward the microphone. "There is evidence that the body is that of a modern woman. We've called in an expert to help us better date the bones, but her dental work is modern, not of the time when the Silverpeak Mine was active."

"What kind of expert?" someone asked.

"A forensic reconstructionist," Butch said. "One of the best. We're very lucky she was available. She should be able to reconstruct our mystery woman's features so that we know what she looked like, which should aid in identifying her."

Another clamor arose as people asked for more details, but Butch only shook his head and stood back. The sheriff took his place. "We're asking the public to come forward if they have any information pertaining to this woman. That's all for now." He turned and left, and

Gage and Butch followed, ignoring the questions called after them.

Caleb and the others became part of the crowd pushing their way out of the room. When they were on the sidewalk, Sheri was the first to speak. "Wow," she said.

"Did you know the body was a modern woman?" Ryan asked Caleb.

"I didn't even know it was a woman," Caleb said. "I mean, it was just a pile of bones. They were clean, except for a lot of dust, so I figured they had to be old."

"I don't remember anything about a missing woman," Sheri said. "Do you?" She asked the question of Tony.

Tony shook his head. "In a town this small, if someone goes missing, people don't forget."

"Butch said that day that the mine would make a good dump site," Sheri said. She hugged herself and rubbed her arms. "It's horrible to think about."

"I guess we'll have to wait to see what this expert says," Ryan said.

"That poor woman," Sheri said. "It wasn't so bad when we thought it was a miner who died a hundred years ago. But a modern-day woman—she probably has family somewhere who are looking for her. At least, I hope she does."

"If this reconstruction expert can really recreate her face, someone will probably recognize her," Ryan said.

"What if she's not from around here?" Sheri asked. "No one we know is missing, after all."

Caleb said nothing, though his stomach was in a knot. *This wasn't Nora*, he told himself. Nora had no reason to be anywhere near Eagle Mountain. Even if she had found out he was living here, she wouldn't have come anywhere near him, knowing how he felt about her. But there had to be a reason the private investigator he had hired hadn't been able to find her since the day she ran off with his new truck and most of his money. The PI had even suggested she might be dead; she had disappeared so completely. But he had never been able to prove that either, leaving Caleb in limbo.

No, he wouldn't be lucky enough to have Nora's body show up here in Eagle Mountain. Not that he really wanted her dead. He wasn't quite that angry anymore. But if she had done to some other man what she had done to him and ended up killed, he couldn't say he would be surprised. Still, he didn't think the body was Nora's. Their situation would never resolve so easily.

DANIELLE DROVE SLOWLY down Eagle Mountain's Main Street. Butch hadn't been kidding when he said the town was like something off a postcard. Victorian storefronts lined the street, many of the windows adorned with flower boxes overflowing with red and white petunias or geraniums. More flowers spilled from baskets hung from light posts, and decorative iron benches at regular intervals along the sidewalks provided a place for weary shoppers to rest. A banner overhead advertised the upcoming Fourth of July celebration.

Mountains rose in the distance, a few patches of snow clinging to the uppermost peaks, the red and yellow scars of mine tailings showing through the dense evergreens on the lower slopes. Butch had promised to take her into the mountains to see the wildflowers. When she had protested that she was coming here to work, he had chided her. "You need a break, don't you?"

Which only added to her suspicions that he had made up his need for her help as a pretext to get her out of the city. She had broken down at that news conference and he had decided she was stressed out—which was certainly true. When she had texted that she was leaving her job, instead of interrogating her about what was wrong, he had manufactured this getaway in his personal mountain paradise. She was touched, but also uneasy. If she stayed with him, she would have to eventually tell him the real reason for leaving her job. Would he think she was a coward for running away? Would he, a lifelong bachelor, even understand why she wanted this baby?

She slowed and consulted the directions he had texted her. "GPS doesn't always work great in these rural areas," he had warned.

She found the road where she needed to turn. Three blocks later she had left the town behind. She drove past fenced pastures with grazing cattle, then through a stand of thick trees and finally, and somewhat surprisingly, into a neighborhood of sprawling lots and houses. Butch's place was down a narrow side road and had a pair of antlers affixed to an archway over the driveway.

She pulled in and parked behind an SUV and a boat. Butch stepped onto the porch before she even got out of the car. He looked the same as always—portly, thinning hair, a little rumpled, but with kind brown eyes and a sympathetic expression. He greeted her with a big hug. When his arms tightened around her, the real tenderness of the gesture brought tears to her eyes. She hastily blinked them away and stepped back, hoping the smile she forced to her lips would convince him that she was all right. "How was the drive?" he asked.

"Long," she said. Too long to be alone with her thoughts, but she chose not to mention that. Instead she turned to look at his house, a low-slung ranch style with a green metal roof. "This is quite a place you have here."

"It suits me. Let's get your things and I'll show you where you'll be staying."

He took the suitcase while she reached into the back seat and withdrew the cat carrier. Butch didn't even blink. "This must be Mrs. Marmalade," he said. He leaned down to peer into the carrier. The cat, an orange-and-black calico, glared back at him and let out an angry yowl.

Butch straightened. "Hopefully she'll be more comfortable inside."

"I brought her litter box and bed and everything." Danielle began to unload these items as well. Between them, she and Butch managed to carry everything. She had been prepared for almost anything, including a futon in the basement, but her temporary quarters turned out to be an efficiency apartment over the garage, complete with a small private deck at the back. "I started to fix it up as a rental, but never got around to listing it," Butch said as he set her suitcase and the cat supplies just inside the doorway. "It's handy for guests, so I use it for that."

She turned from surveying the apartment to face him. "Tell me about this body you need help with," she said.

"You don't have to get to work right away," he said. "You're allowed a day to decompress and relax." The concern in his eyes was genuine, and her eyes stung. She almost broke down and told him everything then and there, but she wasn't quite ready for that.

Instead she assumed a brisk attitude. "I'm dying to hear about this mysterious body you need my help with," she said. "Don't they have forensic reconstructionists on this side of the great divide?"

"None closer than Denver or Salt Lake," he said. "And none as good as you."

"So there really is a body?" she asked. "You didn't make this up as an excuse to get me out here for a visit?"

"There really is a body, and we really do need your help." He smiled, the lines around his eyes creasing like rumpled linen. "Though I'm glad it worked out for you to come."

She settled on the sofa. "Then tell me. I really am interested." And talking about work was another way to avoid telling him about the wreck she had made of her life.

He sat across from her and rubbed his chin.

"It's a puzzler. I don't want to say too much until you've seen her."

"It's a woman, then?" She forced herself to take a deep breath. It was no secret that a lot of her job involved giving faces back to women who had been killed and discarded.

Butch nodded. "I'll take you to her when you've had a chance to get settled."

"I want to see her now," she said. Her initial *meeting* with the victim was always the worst. Though she was used to dealing with bones, decomposing remains were still very unpleasant. But there were important clues to be gleaned from the victim's clothing and other items. Sometimes she could get an idea of hair color. Knowing someone liked bright colored clothing or flashy jewelry helped her form an idea of their personality. Little things could make a difference when it came time to form a final picture.

Butch didn't argue. He pulled keys from his pocket. "I'll drive you."

She set up the litter box, along with food and water, in the apartment's bathroom and locked Mrs. Marmalade in there to get used to the place, then followed Butch out to a large black SUV. He moved a file box, a hat studded with fishing flies and a pair of rubber boots out of the front seat to make room for her. "Looks like you're prepared for anything," she said, and laughed.

"Out here, you have to be," he said.

He drove her into town, to a three-story rock-trimmed building next to the courthouse. "This used to be the county hospital," he said, as he led the way to a side door. "Now it's a medical clinic, but my office and the morgue are in the basement."

The city morgues she had been in were large, antiseptic spaces full of gleaming stainless steel and white porcelain. Butch's morgue was a much more modest affair, a concrete-floored space with a single dissecting table and a small-ish, refrigerated space that would hold, at most, a couple of bodies.

But he didn't move toward the refrigerator, as she had expected. Instead he walked to the counter along the far wall and lifted a light drape that had been covering an array of bones. Most of them were no longer connected, but they were laid out in anatomical order, like the specimens she had studied in school. "She was found like this?" she asked.

"The bones were in a pile in the bottom of the air shaft of an old gold mine in the mountains," Butch said. "The skull was on top. But yes, they were like this. Not a scrap of flesh on them. No clothing or other belongings, either."

She moved closer and studied the bones. They were dry and slightly dusty. None of them appeared to be missing, which was something of a marvel in itself, for bones out in the wild. Animals usually made off with smaller pieces, such as teeth or the small bones of fingers and toes. Maybe a mine shaft was too difficult a place for them to reach. She reached out and touched the humerus, long and perfectly smooth. No remnants of adipose tissue. No gnaw marks from animals. "Someone cleaned these before they were left," she said.

"Cleaned them how?" he asked.

She shrugged. "Boiled them? I can do some tests to try to determine, but I don't think they would be this clean, in this dry climate, unless they had been treated with something." She moved up to the shoulder, and a rougher ridge of bone along the scapula. "She had a break here." She rubbed away the dust to reveal a trio of surgical staples embedded in a ridge of scarring. She traced a path down the left arm to another definite mark. "And here." Screws this time, the heads embedded in the bone. The breaks had healed well. She would look for other injuries, and signs of any past surgeries.

She moved on to the skull, the jaw detached, and several of the teeth arranged on the table beside it. "Modern fillings," she said. She counted five, and one porcelain crown. If someone came forward to identify the woman, they could use dental records to confirm the identification. But they had to have a name first. "Someone wanted to make it hard to identify her," she said.

"I thought the same," Butch said. "Remove the clothing, then remove the possibility of knowing her hair color, or tattoos, or whether or not she had pierced ears." All of those things would decay over time, but it took a long time. Whoever had put this woman in that air shaft wanted to make sure she wouldn't be recognized if she was found sooner rather than later.

"Do you think you'll be able to tell when she died?" Butch asked.

"It depends," she said. The dental work and any surgical evidence could help with dates, but she would have to get lucky to come closer than the last few decades. She traced one finger along the skull, already figuring the measurements she would need to make to begin her reconstruction. "I'll do my best."

A knock on the door interrupted them. "Come in," Butch called.

A good-looking man about her age, with brown eyes fringed with dark lashes, thick brown hair falling over his forehead, stepped into the room.

He glanced at her. "I didn't mean to interrupt," he said, his voice pitched low and soft.

"It's all right. Come on in." Butch waved him over. "Caleb Garrison, this is Danielle Priest. She's a forensic pathologist who specializes in facial reconstruction. One of the best."

"It's nice to meet you, Mr. Garrison," she said, and offered her hand.

"Call me Caleb." They shook hands, his grip warm and gentle. He was over six feet tall, dressed casually in jeans and a T-shirt, lean and muscular, with sharp cheek bones and intense dark eyes. He continued to study her after he released her hand. She tucked her hair behind her ears, conscious that she hadn't even combed it since arriving at Butch's. Had she even remembered to put on mascara this morning?

"Caleb is the man who retrieved the bones from the mine," Butch said. "They were at the bottom of the air shaft and he had to rappel down to them, then climb back up."

"Was there anything else down there with them?" she asked.

He shook his head. "Just the bones." He looked past her, to the table where the skeleton was laid out. "I was at the sheriff's press conference. You think it was a woman?"

"Yes. You can tell from the pelvic bones." She turned and indicated the wide flat bones.

"This notch, called the sciatic notch, is much broader in a woman." She traced one finger along the wide curve at the bottom of the pelvis. "And this section," she moved to the left of the sciatic notch, "is more raised. This is called the auricular surface. You can see it resembles an ear."

He moved in beside her. She caught the scent of clean cotton. "Seeing the bones here, all laid out, they look smaller somehow, more delicate," he said.

"Another indication we're dealing with a female," Danielle said. "Men's bones are generally heavier and thicker. The skulls are different, too. Men have heavier, squarer jaws and bigger foreheads. Once you know what to look for, the differences are obvious."

"Even I recognized them." Butch spoke from behind them. "And I don't have Danielle's training."

"I thought she was probably a miner, a hundred years old or more," Caleb said. "I was sure the bones had been down there a long time because they were so clean."

"She has modern dental work." Danielle nodded to the skull. "And medical screws and staples from surgical repairs. The bones are very clean, but they don't look old. Really old bones are more porous and drier."

"We think someone cleaned these," Butch said.

She felt the shock of this information hit him, the gruesomeness of the idea. *Who would do such a thing?* he was probably thinking, though he said nothing.

"Danielle will be able to reconstruct her face," Butch said. "We'll publish photos and maybe someone will come forward to identify her."

He nodded, still looking stunned.

"Did you need something from me?" Butch asked.

He turned away from the bones. "I saw your car outside and wanted to ask if you knew any more that wasn't said at the press conference. I mean, about who she might be and how she ended up at the mine."

"We may know more when I've had time to examine the skeleton," Danielle said.

"What kind of things can you tell from bones?" he asked, turning back to her.

"Her medical history. And I can probably narrow the age gap. A little about her ethnic background, though that can be trickier."

He nodded.

"Why are you so interested?" Butch asked.

He shrugged. "I guess because I was the one to bring her out of there—it feels more personal. I mean, she could be someone I knew."

"Is someone you know missing?" Butch asked.

He shook his head. "No. But you know how you lose touch with people. Maybe I don't even know they're missing." He took a step back. "I'll let you get back to work." He nodded to Danielle. "It was nice meeting you."

He left. Danielle stared after him. "He seemed pretty upset," she said.

"I was there when he retrieved the bones and he was fine that day," Butch said. "But he's pretty new to search and rescue work. The reality of dealing with a dead body may have hit him later."

She nodded. The work she and Butch and people like them did with the dead was necessary, but she was aware that plenty of people thought she was odd for having chosen this as her profession. The fact that Richard hadn't was one of the things that had drawn her to him.

But she wasn't going to think about Richard.

"Caleb might be able to help you with this project," Butch said.

She frowned. "How could he do that?"

"He knows a lot about local history. He might be able to figure out if this woman had a connection to the mine or one of the former owners."

"I don't solve murders, Butch," she said. "I

only try to determine what she would have looked like when she was alive."

"Of course," he said. "But don't bury yourself here in the lab. This is a beautiful place and you should see some of it while you're here."

"I wouldn't mind seeing the place where this woman was found," she said. She made it a point to never refer to her projects as *remains* or *bones*. They were real people, or at least they had been. She wanted others to remember that.

"Sure. I could arrange that," he said. "Do you think it will help?"

She shrugged. "I don't know. But the more I know about my projects, the better it helps me with reconstruction." She brushed her fingers along the woman's ulna, the bone delicate beneath her fingers. Fragile. Some people thought reconstruction was all about the science of measuring tissue depth and cartilage thickness, plugging numbers into predetermined formulas and translating the results to the skull with clay. But a really good recreation—one that lent personality as well as physical presence to the dead—required imagination and artistry in addition to technical skill. People needed to sense the personality beneath the science. Seeing where this woman had ended up might tell Danielle something about the way her life had ended. That, in turn, might provide a clue to how she had lived.

"Are you ready to get back to the house?" Butch asked.

Alone, she would have chosen to get right to work, but she had her host to consider. And she didn't have any of her supplies with her. "I need just a few more minutes." She pulled her phone from her pocket. "I want to take a few photographs." She liked to document her projects from the very beginning until she had completed the transformation, bone to almost-breath.

"Sure." He jingled his keys in his pocket. "I'll take a walk around the block and meet you back at the truck when you're ready."

He moved away and she might have heard the door close behind him, but the sound barely registered. She was already focused on the woman laid out before her. "Who were you?" she whispered. "What do you have to tell me?"

Chapter Four

Caleb couldn't get away from the morgue fast enough. He hadn't missed the odd looks Danielle and Butch had given him when he had babbled that nonsense about the skeleton possibly belonging to someone he hadn't even known was missing. He felt like a fool, but that was nothing new.

He had only wanted Butch to provide some detail that would prove to him that the skeleton did not belong to Nora. Of course it wasn't her. She had no reason to be in Rayford County, much less up at that old mine. But he had been obsessed with her for far too long. And obsession led to rash behavior—like marrying her in the first place, and now thinking she had turned up here, as if trying to haunt him.

Danielle had said something about surgical screws and staples. Did Nora have those? He honestly didn't know. In the six months they had lived together, the topic of medical histories hadn't come up. Criminal histories, either. What a lot of trouble that would have saved him if he had thought to ask. But how often did that figure into romantic conversations—oh, by the way, have you ever been convicted of fraud? Theft? Larceny?

He rubbed the back of his neck, trying to ease the knot of tension that had taken up permanent residence there in the past year. When Butch had said he was bringing in an expert to help identify the skeleton, Caleb had expected a man Butch's age or older—not an attractive female who appeared to be close to his own age. Danielle Priest wasn't just young, she was beautiful, with a polished city-girl look about her—brown hair expertly cut and streaked with blond, French manicured nails and expensive-looking jeans and tailored shirt. The kind of woman who probably had an equally sophisticated boyfriend back in Denver. It was bad enough that he had made a fool of himself in front of Butch, but bungling so badly in front of her made him feel about two feet tall. Nora had done a pretty good job of crushing his ego, but she hadn't destroyed it entirely.

"Caleb! Wait up a sec."

He turned and suppressed a groan as he saw Butch hurrying toward him. But he stopped and waited. "What's up?" he asked, when Butch stopped in front of him.

Butch pulled a large handkerchief from his pocket and mopped his gleaming forehead. "I was wondering if you'd mind taking Danielle up to the Silverpeak Mine one day? She thinks it would help her with the reconstruction."

"How could it do that?" he asked.

"Danielle works differently than some reconstructionists," Butch said. "She's a scientist, sure, but she's also an artist. Whereas some reconstructions look like mannequins, hers look like people. You can sometimes get good identifications from a mannequin, but you'll get better luck if the picture we run in the paper and distribute to television stations and publish online looks alive."

"And seeing the air shaft where the bones were found will help that?" Caleb asked.

Butch shrugged. "Danielle thinks it will." He glanced back toward the clinic, as if checking to see if Danielle was there. When he turned back to Caleb, he spoke in a softer voice. "She's had a rough time of it, I think. Just left her job. She needed to get away from the city and clear her head. I think it will be good for her to get out a little. A lot of people come here to heal. You know that."

He nodded. People came here to heal. Or

to hide. Depending on the day, he thought he might be doing both. "Sure, I'll take her," he said. "Whenever she wants."

"Thanks. I'll let her know." Butch glanced back over his shoulder again as Danielle emerged from the building. "I'd better go. One of us will be in touch."

Caleb watched Butch as he headed back down the sidewalk. Danielle shaded her eyes with one hand and looked toward them. When she spotted Caleb, her mouth turned down. If he had been a betting man, he would have wagered there was a close to zero chance she would ever call him. Danielle Priest had decided he was someone to avoid. She might even be right about that.

THE FIRST THING Danielle noticed about Rayford County Sheriff Travis Walker when they met on her second day in Eagle Mountain was his looks. The lean dark-haired sheriff had a face made for the big screen, and a magnetism that probably made more than one woman's heart beat faster. Given her own recent experience with handsome powerful men, this might have made her dislike him, but there was nothing arrogant about Sheriff Walker. His manner was respectful, almost courtly. And when he moved in closer, she saw weariness behind the movie-star looks. "I'm sorry to intrude on your work, Ms. Priest," he said after she had admitted him to the morgue, where she was working to glean as much information as possible from the woman's body before transporting the skull to the workshop she and Butch had set up in one bay of the garage below her apartment.

She set aside the calipers she had been using to measure the width of the eye sockets. "That's all right, Sheriff," she said. "How can I help you?"

"I know you haven't started on your reconstruction yet, but I'm hoping you have some information about this woman that we can use to search missing persons databases. If we had some basics—height, age, ethnicity, anything about her medical history—we might be able to come up with some possibilities. From there we could try to match up dental records."

"I can tell you a few things." She picked up a composition book she had been using to record her notes. "The subject is a woman between the age of twenty-five and forty-five. I'd say on the younger end of that age range, based on the fusion of skull sutures and the very minor pitting of the pubic symphysis. I'm going to request analysis of the bone structure of the femur. Based on what we find there, we may be able to pinpoint the age within a few years."

"You can get that close?" he asked.

She nodded. "Younger people have denser bones, and we have enough data at this point to be fairly accurate at pinpointing age based on bone density."

"Anything else you can tell us?" he asked. "Has she given birth?"

She shook her head. "The presence of parturition scars on the pelvis used to be considered an indicator that a woman has given birth, but more recent research has called that into question." She moved to the top of the table and pointed to the staples on the clavicle. "She broke her left shoulder blade, several years premortem, and had surgery to repair the break," she said. "She also broke the radius of her left arm, possibly at the same time. That injury was repaired with six screws."

"What caused the breaks?" he asked.

Danielle shook her head. "An accident? Or maybe abuse?"

"Any idea of her ethnic background?"

"That's trickier. There's a fuzzy ethical line between racial profiling and providing information that's truly helpful." She studied the skull, which lay nestled on a stack of towels at the head of the table. "But I think she was probably white, of northern European ancestry."

He nodded and made a note on his phone.

"Butch told me you think the bones were treated some way to strip them of tissue," he said.

"Yes." She pressed her lips together. "Probably boiled, maybe in a vinegar and water solution. There are signs on some of the longer bones of mild etching, and a few scrape marks, as if with the blade of a knife."

Travis made a face. "Any idea how she was killed?"

"The skull is cracked, but that could have happened postmortem."

Travis nodded again, then stifled a huge yawn. "Sorry," he apologized, and wiped his hand down his face. "We have new twins. I'm not getting much sleep."

Twins! She felt a little dizzy at the idea and resisted the urge to press her hand to her abdomen. *How did your wife do it?* she wanted to ask. Instead she forced a smile. "Congratulations. Boys or girls?"

He couldn't quite suppress a smile. "One of each. With healthy appetites. Keeping us up at night. But they tell me it gets better in a few months." He turned his gaze back to the skeleton. "When were the bones thrown into that shaft?"

"I don't think they were thrown," she said. "If that was the case, they would have scattered on impact. From what I was told about how they were found, and the pictures I was shown, I think they were lowered down there, possibly in some kind of sling. They were too neatly arranged, from the pictures Caleb Garrison took." Butch had presented her with a full set of the crime scene photos that morning.

The sheriff pocketed his phone once more. "We'll put this out on NamUs and see if we get a match. We don't have a record of any local missing women in our files."

She nodded. The National Missing and Unidentified Persons System was the logical place to start the search for a description that matched their Jane Doe. "Maybe we'll get lucky and find a match," she said. Not likely, with no detailed physical description to go on, but she would do her best to provide that.

"What's the next step for you?" the sheriff asked.

"We'll do the bone density studies. I could attempt to retrieve DNA from bone marrow, but that's very iffy, and expensive."

"Hold off on the marrow," he said. "Let's see if the reconstruction yields any results."

"All right." She hesitated, then asked, "Have you found out anything more? Any idea how she ended up at that mine?"

"Not yet. I did a search for similarities to

other crimes—a clean skeleton dumped at a remote site. But I didn't find anything."

"In a way, that's good, I guess." Maybe this wasn't a habitual killer.

"Not to rush you, but how long before you have a face?" the sheriff asked.

"A week to ten days, usually. Maybe sooner. I'll get started on that later today probably."

"Thank you." He nodded and left.

She turned back to the woman's skeleton. She had cleaned the dust from the bones and in doing so had learned one was missing after all—the ring finger of the left hand. Had some small rodent scurried off with it, or had it been lost in transit from wherever the killer processed the body to that mine shaft? Had the killer kept it even, as a grisly souvenir? She had forgotten to mention this to the sheriff, but she would be sure to include this information in her report.

She shuddered, and studied the tableau once more. Her more analytically minded colleagues would have mocked her for her practice of sitting with the bones this way, as if in the silence surrounding them, she might hear the victim say something to reveal who she was and what had happened to her. But all she heard in the long minutes that followed was the cycling on and off of the refrigeration unit's compressor. The bones themselves had little more to reveal either—no gouges from knives or deflected bullets. No crushing or fragmenting from a vicious blow. However this woman had died, it did not appear to have affected her bones, unless the skull fracture had led to her death. There was no way of knowing.

Had the broken bones been because of an accident, or abuse? Had her killer been a romantic partner who had battered her for years, then gone too far? Or was her killer someone she hadn't known well, or a stranger she had never seen before he targeted her? Was a lover or a spouse even now mourning her, wondering what had become of her?

So many questions. And she might never have the answers to any of them. Though she had labored long and hard to resurrect the faces of other murder victims, and found justice for many of them, not every project garnered results. Some of the faces she had reconstructed were part of NamUs files, still waiting for someone who recognized them to come forward.

"I'll do my best for you," she said softly. A promise she made every person who became hers to reveal. She picked up a set of calipers and set to work.

CALEB ENDED HIS online class early on Tuesday to respond to a report of a Jeep rollover accident on a popular trail above Poughkeepsie Gulch. He and the other volunteers arrived at the scene fifty minutes after the call for help to find a red Jeep Rubicon on its side fifty feet below a technical section of the trail that required following a narrow rocky ledge. A trio of four-wheel drive vehicles were parked on either side of the ledge, half a dozen people gathered around a white-haired couple. The man lay on his back, a folded jacket beneath his head and a younger man kneeling beside him. A woman—the man's wife—sat beside him and held her husband's hand, her face almost the same shade as her hair.

Paramedic Hannah Richards hurried to the man's side, medical kit in hand. Caleb and the others followed. The kneeling man stood. "I'm Doctor Frank Terry," he said. "My brother and I were right behind the Samuels when the accident happened."

"What's the situation, Doctor?" Hannah asked as she knelt and took out a stethoscope.

"I'm a dermatologist," Terry said. "But I think he's in cardiac distress."

Hannah listened to the man's chest while he stared up at her with wide frightened eyes. "Mr. Samuel, I'm Hannah, a paramedic and a volunteer with Search and Rescue," she said. "How are you feeling?"

"My chest hurts and…and I'm dizzy." He gripped her hand. "Am I going to die?"

"We're going to do everything we can to prevent that." She turned to Caleb. "Get the oxygen, and we'll need a litter to transport. We'll take him down in the Beast."

Caleb ran for the oxygen and carried it back to Hannah while the others reconfigured the inside of the Beast to serve as a backcountry ambulance. The specially outfitted Jeep had the high clearance and short wheelbase capable of negotiating these steep four-wheel-drive trails. "Do you have any other injuries?" she was asking when Caleb returned.

"I banged my knee when I jumped out of the Jeep," Mr. Samuel said.

Hannah moved to check the knee, which had a bloody scrape but was already scabbing over. "That doesn't look too bad. I'm going to put this oxygen mask on now. I want you to breathe normally for me and try to relax." She adjusted the mask, checked the pulse oximeter she had clipped to Mr. Samuel's finger, then addressed Mrs. Samuel, asking about medications and medical history. "We're going to take your husband down to the main highway," she said. "A medical helicopter will meet us there and take him to the hospital in Junction."

"Is he going to be all right?" she asked, her voice quavering.

"It's a great sign that he's still conscious and responsive," Hannah said. "And he had a doctor with him right away." She looked up as a group approached with the litter. "Caleb is going to talk to you about what happened while we get your husband ready for his ride down the mountain."

Caleb moved in to help Mrs. Samuel to her feet. He turned her away from her husband, leaving the others free to tend to him. "You weren't hurt in the accident?" he asked.

"No." She glanced back over her shoulder at the group around her husband.

"He's in good hands," Caleb said.

She searched his face, then nodded. "Thank you all so much," she said.

"Tell me what happened," Caleb said.

"When we got to this section, I was so scared I got out of the Jeep and said I would walk." Her lips trembled, but she pressed them together and breathed deeply, then continued. "Darryl insisted he could do this." She made a tsking sound. "The Jeep is new and he thinks he knows everything. I told him he takes too many chances, and now look what happened."

"He said something about jumping out,"

Caleb said, before she could spiral into accusations.

"Yes. The Jeep started to slip sideways. I saw it happening and shouted for him to stop. I don't even know if he heard me, but the next thing I knew, the Jeep went one way and Darryl went the other. I was so relieved he was alive. He wasn't even hurt—just a scraped knee. But he was beside himself. He kept saying, *My new Jeep! My new Jeep*! Then he just... He just fell over." Her face crumpled and she covered her mouth with her hand and let out a sob.

Caleb put his arm around her. "That must have been terrifying," he said. "But the worst is over now." He glanced back to see the others sliding the litter into the back of the Beast. "Let's go back and you can ride down with Darryl."

He saw her safely loaded into the Beast and headed down the mountain. They began gathering their equipment. The other Jeepers started to move away. "Hey, guys," Hannah called after them. "Can you give us a ride down?" They had all ridden up in the Beast, which hadn't had room for them on the return trip.

Jake and Caleb ended up riding in the back seat of an FJ Cruiser with two middle-aged sisters from Nevada who peppered him with questions about working search and rescue. "What you do is so wonderful, saving lives," the sister with short curly hair, who introduced herself as Doreen, said.

"You're obviously in terrific shape," the other half of the duo, Maureen, who wore her hair in a low ponytail, said this as she eyed Caleb's legs in a pair of hiking shorts.

"Yes, ma'am," he said, assuming the serious demeanor of a trained professional.

"What's the scariest rescue you've been on?" Doreen asked.

Jake tilted his head, considering. "I guess for me, it's anything having to do with bees," he said.

Caleb and the two women stared at him. "Bees?" Doreen asked.

"Yeah. One time we responded to a wreck on the pass. A truck hauling a bunch of beehives blew a tire and crashed into a snowshed. It was awful."

Maureen looked back at them, her face a mask of concern. "How horrible. Were the injuries very awful?"

"Oh, the driver of the truck was fine," Jake said. "And most of the bees were fine. But I hope I never have a call like that again. It was terrifying." He shuddered.

"Why was that?" Doreen asked.

Jake shrugged. "What can I say? I'm allergic to bees."

Caleb bit the inside of his cheek to keep from laughing. The women fell silent after that. Jake kept a straight face the rest of the way down the mountain, but as soon as they were back at Search and Rescue headquarters, out of sight of the sisters, both men burst out laughing.

"What was all that about bees?" Caleb asked.

"I'm not really allergic," Jake said. "But I was tired and didn't feel like telling war stories. That seemed like a polite way to shut them down."

Caleb nudged his shoulder. "You are such a dork." Then he sobered. "Has the sheriff's department found out anything about the woman whose skeleton we found at the Silverpeak Mine?"

Jake shook his head. "We ran the information we got from the forensic pathologist through the national registry of missing persons but there are so many women in that age range, of similar heights and ages, who have vanished. Until we have more information, it's impossible to find a match."

The other volunteers had arrived back at headquarters by now and they spent the next half hour organizing and repacking equipment in preparation for the next mission. "While you're all here, I need to let you know we're going to get a visit from observers from the Mountain Rescue Association," Sheri announced. "They'll be evaluating our performance as part of the process of recertifying us for another five years. Those of you who have been with the group for a while know the drill, and may even know the evaluators. For the rest of you, just perform your duties as usual. These are all experienced backcountry rescue pros and they're here to help us improve our performance, as much as to test us. Answer any questions they ask honestly, and if you don't know something, don't be afraid to admit it."

"Treat them like any fellow volunteer," Tony said. "I've never been shy about asking them to pitch in if we need help. If they're experts, we might as well take advantage of their expertise."

"Good point," Sheri said. "You rookies could learn from these people, so if you get the opportunity, seize it. But don't let them do your work for you. They want to see how we handle tough situations. I'm confident we don't have anything to worry about. We're a solid team, and we have plenty of experience."

"We'll do our best to impress," long-time volunteer Danny Irwin said.

"Just do your normal excellent job and you won't have anything to worry about," Sheri said.

They finished packing the gear. Caleb was waiting on a group that planned to head to Mo's Pub for dinner when his phone rang. He stepped away to answer it. "Hello?"

"Mr. Garrison?" asked a pleasant woman's voice. "This is Connie Schaeffer, with All Points Investigations."

He had a vague memory of a grandmotherly redhead who had taken notes in the investigator's office when Caleb had hired the firm to track down Nora. "Yes, this is he," Caleb said.

"You asked for an update on our search for Nora Garrison."

"Or Nora Shapiro," he said. That was her maiden name. Surely she wasn't still using his name. "Have you found her?"

"If we had found her, we would have contacted you immediately," Connie said. "But I promise you, we are still looking. Mr. Phillips asked me to pass on that he has recently had a very credible lead showing that Ms. Shapiro was in Thornton, Colorado, in March of this year."

Caleb felt as if he were choking. He struggled to breathe. The last time he had talked to Phillips, the PI had said he had tracked Nora to Phoenix, Arizona, where she was working as a waitress in a sports bar—the same job she had had when Caleb met her. She had left that job four months ago and disappeared. "What was she doing back in Colorado?" he asked.

"She told the coworker Mr. Phillips talked to that she was looking for you."

Chapter Five

Danielle studied the 3D scan of Jane Doe's skull on her computer screen. The program computed the correct depth and location for all the markers she needed to place before she began applying the first clay. The markers provided a guideline to the thickness and contours of the flesh at various points on the skull. As she filled in between the markers with layers of clay, a unique face would gradually be revealed.

She turned away from the computer, toward the skull itself. Last night she had mounted it onto a neck she had sculpted from plaster of Paris. The effect was of an all-white sculpture, elegant for all she still lacked most of her features. Danielle had attached the mandible with wax and replaced the few teeth that had fallen out, and filled the eye sockets with glass eyes. Now the woman resembled the Day of the Dead icons popular in Mexico—something to be celebrated, not feared.

During the course of her work, Danielle came to know her subjects. She hoped that if there was an afterlife, this woman looked kindly on her efforts to care for her and restore her to some dignity. As she had cradled the skull and set it gently on the neck, she felt a wave of tenderness. Maybe because she was working alone in this unfamiliar place. Maybe because she too had felt abandoned, as were all the people she worked to bring to life again.

She stood, one hand pressed to the small of her back, which ached. She straightened and smoothed her loose shirt over a pair of black leggings. She could only wear her blue jeans right now if she left the top button undone. When she stood in front of the full-length mirror in the apartment's bedroom, she could detect a definite bump in her abdomen. The doctor she had seen in Denver had informed her that her probable due date was about November 14. That had seemed so far in the future at the time, but was it really enough time to do all the things she needed to do to get ready?

She needed to start by confiding in Butch. He had been scrupulous about not asking her what had happened back in Denver, but the way he studied her when he thought she was unaware showed how concerned he was. And maybe having someone else know would make her feel less alone and bewildered.

She let out a snort of laughter. Not that Butch was going to know much about pregnancy and babies. He was a doctor, yes, but she wasn't really looking for clinical advice. She wanted another woman to reassure her that she could do this intimidating thing. She could grow a new life inside herself and take care of it after it was born. And she could do it all alone.

But she didn't have a sister or even a sister-in-law to talk to. Her mother and father had both died in their early fifties, when she was scarcely twenty. Losing them both so suddenly had been one more factor in her breakdown.

She started to turn back toward the computer, then stopped and looked out the window. The sun was shining in the kind of sky children draw—bright blue heavens with fluffy white clouds. A few minutes in the fresh air would revive her spirits and probably help ease her back pain, too.

She walked up the drive and turned onto the street. Butch's house was near the end, in a neighborhood of large lots, each house separated from its neighbors by thick woods. This time of day—midafternoon—all was quiet. Everyone was probably at work, she thought, and stopped and closed her eyes a moment, savoring a peace only enhanced by a few bars of birdsong from a robin in a nearby spruce.

When she opened her eyes again, she was surprised to see a woman walking toward her. "Hello," the woman called when she was still some distance away.

"Hello," Danielle replied. She thought they would pass by each other without further comment, but the woman stopped beside Danielle, out of breath. She was a petite blonde with a definite baby bump rounding her abdomen. She noticed Danielle staring and smiled and rubbed a protective hand across her belly. "My doctor says it's good for me to get out and walk, but I get so winded, you know?"

Danielle nodded. She got out of breath every time she climbed the steps to her apartment, or even up a slight incline, but she had thought that was due to the altitude. "Is that usual for pregnant women?" she asked. "To get out of breath?"

"My doctor tells me it is." The woman smiled down at her belly. "This is my first."

"When are you due?"

"September 17."

So eight weeks or so further along than Danielle. And a lot bigger. How much longer would Danielle be able to hide her own condition? Not that she was ashamed or anything. She wanted this baby. But people would have questions, chief among them being where is the baby's father?

"Do you mind if we walk together?" the woman asked. "I usually turn around about here."

"No, I'd enjoy the company." Danielle moved over to make more room on the side of the road. Not that there was any traffic.

"I'm Carissa," the woman said. "Carissa Miller. My husband, Joey, and I live in that green house at the end of the street."

"I'm Danielle Priest. I'm staying in the apartment over Butch Collins's garage."

"He's the coroner, right?"

"Yeah," Danielle said.

Carissa hugged herself. "Kind of a creepy job, right?"

"Butch isn't creepy, though," Danielle said. What would this woman think if she knew what Danielle did for a living?

"Oh, no, he's always seemed really nice." Carissa pushed a thick sweep of blond curls off her face. She had dark roots, and Danielle couldn't help noticing her fingernails were bitten almost to the quick. "Are you new to the area? I don't think I've seen you around before."

"I'm just visiting," Danielle said.

"Oh." Carissa pouted. "I was hoping you had moved in. It would be nice to have someone near my own age around." She gestured to indicate the houses they were passing. "Most of the people along here are retired." She laughed. "I've introduced myself to my next-door neighbor three times now and she never can remember my name. She's called me Melissa, Carolyn and Francisca."

"Other than the breathlessness, how are you doing?" Danielle asked. She couldn't help it — she had so many questions about what to expect as her own body changed. Looking up information on the internet wasn't the same as talking to another woman.

"Oh, you know, the usual. The first three months I was so sick, but that got better. And tired! There are days I'm fine and other days I can hardly get out of bed. Joey doesn't understand, but I just tell him it takes a lot of energy to grow a whole other human."

Danielle nodded. She hadn't struggled too terribly with morning sickness, but she had battled fatigue. She hadn't been sure how much of her weariness was due to the baby and how much to depression over Richard.

"Is your husband excited about the baby?" Danielle asked.

"He says he is but you know how men are.

They never show their emotions the way women do. He's the strong silent type, which is one of the things that attracted me to him." She laughed again. "I tell him I talk enough for both of us." She stopped at the end of a driveway lined with tall blue spruce. "This is my place. It was nice meeting you. Maybe we can walk together again some time."

"I'd like that," Danielle said.

She scarcely noticed the scenery as she walked back to Butch's, her mind too full of thoughts of her baby and what the future might hold. Next time she saw Butch, she would tell him about the baby, and maybe about Richard, too. She hoped he would understand why she didn't want to fight Richard. She only wanted to be left in peace to raise her child. She didn't need Richard to interfere.

She was so preoccupied with these plans that she didn't notice the man waiting in front of the garage until he stepped out of the shadows and moved toward her. She stopped a few feet away, her heart pounding beneath the hand she pressed to her chest. "You startled me," she said to Caleb Garrison.

"I'm sorry," he said. "I hope now isn't a bad time, but I was hoping you had a few minutes to talk."

"Sure. Come in."

She unlocked the door to her studio and he moved past her to the worktable, where he stood staring at the still-naked skull mounted on the plaster neck. "I would have thought you would do the eyes last," he said.

"I like to do them first." She shrugged. "I think they make her look more human."

"Why did you choose brown?"

"It's the most common eye color, so a good default."

"What's the next step?" he asked, continuing to study the skull.

She moved up beside him. "We know from research the depth of tissue at various points on the skull and we use those measurements to map the general contours of the face," she said. "A computer program does that, then I place markers to guide me. Bony protrusions on the skull where the muscles were attached in life give us clues as to the markers' placement. The nose and lips have to be added, but they're the most subjective part. That tissue is too fragile to survive decomposition, so I make my best estimate, using what clues I can glean from the skull itself. After they're applied, I move on to ears and eyelids. I'll fill in the clay to the depths indicated by markers and finish off with a thin layer of tinted clay for the skin.

Last is the wig and again, I have to guess at the hair color and style."

"So you use science, but a lot of it is guess-work," he said.

"I prefer to think of it as instinct." She looked into the eyes of the skull before her. She couldn't yet see the woman Jane Doe had been, but she would. Call it intuition or divine guidance or some kind of extra-sensory perception, but she had shown a knack for creating reconstructions that uncannily resembled the living people the bones had once belonged to. "I can never be a hundred percent sure of my choices," she said. "But I have a good track record of reconstructing an image her relatives and friends will be able to recognize."

"I'm impressed," Caleb said. He moved away from the skull, examining the rest of the room. She had fashioned a makeshift studio with a worktable and shelves for her supplies—wire for armatures, clear jars of colored rubber markers the size and shape of pencil erasers, glues, wax, glass eyes, clay and pigments.

"What did you want to talk to me about?" she asked. She could feel his agitation, a nervous energy filling the room like incense.

"I wanted to see how the reconstruction was going."

She didn't think that was true. Or not entirely. "You looked upset when you first got here," she said.

"I'm anxious to know who she is," he said.

That rang true. "Why?" she asked. "Do you think you know her?"

"Maybe."

She gaped. "You think you know who this is and you haven't said anything until now?"

He raked a hand through his hair, the corded muscles of his forearms standing out. "I don't know who she is," he said. "I just… It's complicated."

"Maybe you should be talking to the sheriff."

He lowered his hand and his eyes met hers. They were a very dark brown, deep set with fine lines fanning out from the corners and full of such pain her throat clenched in sympathy. "I'd rather tell you," he said. "If you're in the mood to hear a wild story."

She wasn't going to let him walk out after a line like that. She moved to the bar stool she had set up in front of the workbench and indicated its mate across from her. "Tell me."

He perched on the edge of the stool, one foot on the bottom rung of the support, the other braced on the floor, as if poised to leap up at any second. "Nothing about this story makes me look good," he said. "I don't have any excuses, except to say that I must have lost my mind there for a little while."

She nodded, but kept quiet, sensing he was gathering his courage. He blew out a breath. "Just under two years ago, I met a woman at a sports bar in Denver where I used to hang out," he said. "She and I really hit it off." He stared at the floor. "I was stupid about her, really. We started dating and after a couple of weeks she moved in with me. I think part of me knew it was too soon, but she had lost her lease and I know how hard it can be to find a place and she said she wanted us to be together all the time. I wanted that, too. And everything was going great. After a month she told me she thought she was pregnant."

Danielle choked off a gasp and hoped Caleb hadn't heard. He kept his gaze on the floor. "I was in shock," he said. "I mean, that's not anything I had expected, because she had told me she was on birth control. I said maybe it was too soon to tell, but she showed me a positive test and said her doctor had confirmed it. Then she started crying and accused me of not wanting the baby. I told her no, no, I was happy, just surprised." He grimaced. "The thing was, after the initial shock wore off, I really was happy. I've always liked kids and I thought it would be great to be a dad."

He fell silent. She leaned forward, scarcely breathing. He had talked about his girlfriend, but never a child. "What happened to the baby?" she asked, her voice just above a whisper.

"There was no baby." His voice had hardened, each word spoken as if it tasted bitter. "There never was a baby. But I didn't know that until later. In that moment, I was happy and I wanted her to be happy. I asked her to marry me. We flew to Las Vegas, got married in a chapel there and flew home two days later. I had to leave the next week to go to Cambridge for a six-month stint as a guest lecturer. The plan was for her to follow as soon as she got her passport. She drove me to the airport and kissed me goodbye. And that's the last time I ever saw her."

Danielle blinked. "What happened?"

"We talked every night. She was full of news about how she was packing her things and planning to be with me, how the pregnancy was progressing. I fell for every bit of it. I was looking for a place to rent that had room for a nursery, but every time the date when she was supposed to join me drew near, something happened to delay her arrival. At first her passport application was delayed. Then some of the paperwork had been lost and she had to send in more documentation. She told me because she had changed her name when we married it was taking longer than usual. It was frustrating, but I was sure we would be together, and she told me constantly how much she wanted to be with me. The weeks turned into months. I'd been in England four months when a colleague suggested I talk to the American consulate. The consulate's office promised to do what they could to expedite the application. When I told Nora, I was sure she would be thrilled. Instead, she told me I was only going to foul things up further, that she had everything under control. Then I told her I was going to fly home the next weekend because I had a break in the schedule. I thought she would be thrilled about that, too. Instead, she said I shouldn't waste the expense of a ticket, especially when we wanted to save for a house, and she was sure we would be together soon, et cetera, et cetera." He shook his head. "I bought it all. I believed every word she said, and that she really wanted us to be together."

Danielle said nothing, but waited with a growing sense of dread.

He blew out a breath. "Anyway, the consulate got back to me and said he couldn't find any record of a passport application for Eleanor Shapiro or Eleanor Garrison. Nothing. I called Nora and told her and she started crying. She said she couldn't believe this was happening, after all we had been through. I spent most of the call trying to calm her down. I was upset, too—so upset I thought about cutting my work in Cambridge short. At least she talked me out of that—it wouldn't have done my reputation any good to walk out on a plum position like that. So, we decided we would just wait. I only had about six weeks left before I could come home. We would be together then. But when I did finally make it home, Nora was gone. Along with my new truck and all the money in my bank account."

"She took everything?" Danielle asked.

He nodded, his expression grim. "As soon as we were married, I made her a joint account holder and put her name on the truck title, too. She persuaded me that since I was going to be out of the country, having her name on everything would make it easier for her to handle all my affairs. She handled them all right."

"What did you do?"

"I contacted the police right away. At first I thought she was just missing. I was worried about her, and about the baby. They interviewed the neighbors and found out that I hadn't been gone long before Nora moved another man into the apartment with her. They had had a great time driving my truck and spending my money.

My next-door neighbor had seen her in a bikini and she definitely wasn't pregnant. I'll never forget the pitying look the cop gave me when he told me all this."

Danielle pitied him too, though she tried not to show it. "What did you do?"

"I spent a lot of time taking her off my accounts. She had run up a lot of bills on my credit cards that I had allowed her access to. I had to close all the accounts. I got a job with a carpet-cleaning company working nights just to pay some bills, and taught my classes during the day. I was miserable and ashamed and in a pretty dark place."

Danielle nodded. She had been there, too. "How did you end up in Eagle Mountain?" she asked.

"A friend teaches at Colorado State. He had heard through the grapevine about what happened and reached out to tell me there was an opening for a history prof. Not great pay, but enough. I was planning on getting a place in Junction, but I came here one weekend, to try to clear my head. I saw the place I'm in for rent and decided to take it. I've been climbing off and on for years, but here I really got serious about it. I liked the challenge and it helped me get in shape and clear my head. A friend I met climbing told me Search and Rescue was looking for volunteers who were climbers, so I volunteered. I thought maybe saving other people was better than sitting around, beating myself up. And it's helped."

Danielle turned to the skull on the workbench. "What makes you think this is Nora?" she asked.

"I don't think it's her," he said. "Why would she have been up at that mine? Or anywhere on this side of the divide? But I hired a private investigator to find her. Not because I wanted to see her again, but I do want a divorce, and for that I need to know where to send the papers. For months, he wasn't able to come up with anything. It was as if she just disappeared." He blew out a breath. "But yesterday I talked to his office. He had tracked her back to the Front Range. A coworker he talked to said she was looking for me. I wouldn't be hard to find. I'm listed online as part of the faculty of Colorado State. What if she came here to find me and ended up getting killed?"

"It would be a wild coincidence," Danielle said.

"Everything about this story is wild." He sat back. "The investigator I hired said it looked like Nora planned the whole scam from the first, maybe with her boyfriend's help. She heard me talking about leaving the country and made it a point to go after me. And I was dumb enough to fall for it."

"It's hard to see people clearly when you're infatuated," she said. In the early days of her relationship with Richard, she had believed so many good things about him that turned out to not be true.

"This was more than infatuation," he said. "I lost my mind for a while there."

"I'm sorry that happened to you," she said.

He straightened. "I didn't come here to unload all this on you," he said. "But do you see why I can't go to the sheriff with this? Yeah, the investigator I hired can't find Nora, but that's probably because she doesn't want to be found. She's probably alive and well and scamming some other gullible guy. But I don't *know* that for sure, and now this woman turns up…" He looked over his shoulder at the skull and grimaced. "Nora has blue eyes."

"If you know the name of her dentist, we could compare her dental records," Danielle said.

"I don't know her dentist. Or her doctor. I don't know her blood type or even if her hair was really blond or if she dyed it. I only spent a little over a month with her, total. And a lot of that time was in bed. She made sure of that." He met her gaze, his expression pleading. "I never did anything that impulsive before," he said.

"Is the investigator still looking for her?" she asked.

"Yes. I still want that divorce, though I'll probably never trust myself enough to marry again." He stood. "Please don't tell anyone about this. One of the reasons I like it here is that no one knows what a giant fool I made of myself."

"I won't tell."

"When you have her face, will you let me see it?" he asked. "If it is Nora, I promise I'll go straight to the sheriff and tell him everything."

"All right." She walked with him to the door. She wanted to say something to make him feel better. He had been naive, but was it really worse than things other people had done under the influence of what they thought was love? "I think everyone has made mistakes in relationships," she said. "Some are worse than others, but that's part of being human."

"Yeah, well, I've learned my lesson," he said. He opened the door and turned back. "I almost forgot. Butch said you wanted to see where the bones were found."

"Where *she* was found. She was a real person, not just a skeleton." She and Richard had argued this point, he accusing her of being pedantic.

"Of course. Where she was found. I can take you, whenever you want to go."

She had meant for Butch to take her, but obviously he had passed that chore onto Caleb. "All right. Would tomorrow work?" If she didn't make a commitment now, she would continue to put it off in favor of devoting herself to the project. It was an old habit, one she felt she should break.

"Tomorrow, then. I have a morning class, but I'm free after that. Unless I get a search and rescue call."

They set a time and he left. Danielle returned to her workshop, but Caleb's story had unsettled her. How different his reaction than Richard's to the news that he might be a father. How different her life might have been if Richard had welcomed the idea of a baby.

But would that really have been a good thing? Richard would still be Richard. Now that the fog of infatuation had lifted, she could see more of what her life with him would have been like. His ambition and goals would always have come before her happiness or that of their children. He was a man who used other people to get what he wanted.

Caleb had been used too, more cruelly than

she had been. She returned to the workbench and studied the skull. The odds of this woman being Nora had to be very low. But life was full of odd circumstances. What if Caleb's search for the woman who had hurt him could end here?

She picked up a handful of round rubber markers and rolled them around in her palm, then began to carefully place them on the skull.

Chapter Six

Caleb had thought telling Danielle his story would make him feel worse, reliving his shame. But it hadn't been that way at all. She had listened calmly, sympathetic, but without trying to make excuses for his behavior or being too critical, either. Maybe that was what confession was like, unburdening yourself to someone who promised forgiveness. Not that Danielle had anything to forgive him for. But he did feel lighter now. And he was glad she knew the reason for his interest in the woman from the mine. They could be more comfortable together. She seemed like a nice woman, and he would enjoy showing her around the area while she was here.

The next afternoon, he drove with her to the Silverpeak Mine. She had dressed for the outing in hiking boots, a long-sleeved T-shirt and jeans. She was more petite than Nora, less curvy and her hair was dark, not blond. Not that it mattered, but he thought her being so unlike his ex made it easier to be with her. How long was he going to keep comparing other women to Nora? He didn't like it, but he couldn't seem to help it.

"This is beautiful," she said, as he guided his truck—a battered Chevy he had purchased cheaply to replace the tricked-out Ford Nora had made off with—up the narrow forest service road toward the mine. Mountains rose on all sides, stands of aspen interspersed with clumps of fir and spruce so thick they looked almost black against the turquoise sky, and high meadows carpeted with wildflowers. "Or do you take it for granted, living here all the time?" she asked.

"Never." He shook his head. "For one thing, it's always different. Different flowers, different sky, changing colors and weather. I was up here in winter and everything was buried in snow."

"Maybe all that snow is why the wildflowers are so pretty now."

He slowed to turn onto the rutted track that led up to the mine. "This is private property but I called earlier and the owners said it was okay if I brought you up here," he said. "They were pretty upset about finding those bones— that woman—and want to do everything they can to help figure out who she was and why she was there."

He parked at the end of the drive, in a clearing near a new foundation and stacks of lumber, and he and Danielle got out. "The owners are building a cabin and plan to make this a summer home," he said.

"Are they going to mine?" Danielle asked. "Butch said it was a gold mine."

"It was. Not a profitable one, from the research I've been able to do. So many of these small operations weren't." He pulled a pack from behind the seat and slipped it on. They weren't going far, but he had responded to enough hiking accidents to know the wisdom of carrying water, snacks and basic first-aid supplies on even a short trek on these rough trails. "Some people buy up these places to mine, but most people are just looking for less expensive land. There aren't any county services up here, no good sources of water and it's inaccessible in the winter, unless you want to get here on skis or snowshoes or a snowmobile. They use the places as summer getaways, primarily. Besides, the main tunnel of this mine is collapsed. It would take a lot of work to dig it out."

He started up a trail at the end of the driveway. Danielle fell in behind him. Soon she was breathing heavily from the steep climb. At the top of the ridge, he stopped and waited for her. "I forgot you haven't lived at altitude very long," he said. "I'll take it easier from now on."

"You're...not even...breathing hard," she said.

"I do a lot of training," he said. "Trail running and weights, climbing. We respond to a lot of accidents in remote places and you have to be in shape."

"Hmm." She pulled a water bottle from her pack and drank, but he noticed she was looking him over. He wondered if she liked what she saw, then immediately dismissed the thought. What did he care?

"Where is the mine?" she asked, looking around them.

"Over there." He pointed along the ridge ahead of them. "You can see the mine waste spilling down this slope—all that orange and yellow rock. And that pile of timbers used to be the entrance to the main adit—the tunnel where they mined the ore."

"Where is the shaft where my Jane Doe was found?"

"Beyond that."

She stowed her water bottle. "Let's go."

They walked another ten minutes along the ridge, skirting the pile of weathered timbers and rusty tin that was all that remained of the adit, to what at first appeared to be just a low rim of rock slightly downhill. "This is an air shaft to carry fresh air into the tunnel," Caleb explained. "Not all of them are this elaborate. Sometimes the miners used stovepipe."

"I didn't even know mines had air shafts." She peered down into the hole, which was about three feet across.

"Not all of them do, but if you have very long tunnels it's good to get fresh air inside. Bad gases can build up—methane and stuff. People die when that happens." He dug a flashlight from his pack and handed it to her. "Here. Shine this down in there."

She did so, revealing the dusty bottom of the shaft, empty except for a few dried leaves. "She was down there?"

"Yes, in a neat pile almost directly under the opening."

She returned the flashlight to him. "How did anyone ever see her?"

"The owners wanted to put a metal grate over this opening, to keep animals or people from falling in. When they came up with the grate, they looked in and saw the bones. When they realized they were human, they called the sheriff, who called Search and Rescue, because we had the climbing gear to get her out."

"And you were the one to do it."

"Probably any of our team could have done it," he said. "It's not a difficult climb. But I was the first to volunteer." He glanced into the shaft again. "I'm still a rookie, proving myself, I guess. This was a no-pressure situation, so good practice."

"And I'm impressed you climbed down in there. It must have been like lowering yourself into a well."

"I don't get claustrophobic," he said. "But it's okay with me if I don't have to do anything like that again. Rescues are a lot more satisfying when you can actually help someone."

"You helped Jane Doe. You brought her out into the world so people could know about her."

"And so you could give her a face."

"I always hope knowing who she is will help find her killer," Danielle said. "But sometimes it's enough for the families to know where their missing daughter or wife or mother ended up. It's sad, but they tell me it's better than never knowing."

"That's how I feel about Nora," he said. "I want to know what happened to her so I can serve her with papers and sever my ties to her altogether. Until that happens, I feel stuck."

"The odds aren't very high that Jane Doe is her," Danielle said.

"I know. But it will be one more thing to

cross off the list. The PI is still looking for her. Maybe he'll catch a break and locate her."

"You said the investigator you hired told you she was looking for you," Danielle said. "Would you talk to her if she found you?"

He shook his head. "I have a lot of things I'd like to say to her, but I'm not sure I could keep my temper in check enough to say them. It's better I stay away from her."

"Are you afraid she'd talk you into getting back together?"

He laughed, but there was no mirth in the sound. "Not a chance."

She walked a little away from the shaft and stared out over the valley. "Someone would have to know this shaft was there," she said. "This wasn't just a random dumping site."

"Her killer, you mean," he said.

"The person who put her there, but yes, that was probably her killer."

"You said before that he, well, cleaned off the bones." He didn't want to think about what that had entailed.

"Yes. It would make it more difficult to identify her. No clothing, no hair, no tattoos or other marks," she said. "So he's either local or has spent enough time here to know about this place."

"I'm not sure how many locals know about

this," he said. "I didn't, though I've only been in the area less than a year."

"What about the people who bought the mine?" she asked.

He shook his head. "The Krupkes are a couple in their sixties, from Houston. I'm not saying they couldn't have done something like this, but they were the ones who reported it to the sheriff, and they seem genuinely freaked out about it and want to help."

"The sheriff says there haven't been any local women reported missing."

"No." He moved in beside her. "I asked the Krupkes if they've ever encountered anyone else on the property and they said no, but they're not here most of the time. It probably wouldn't have been that hard for someone to come up here when he knew they were back in Houston. Like you said, it's pretty remote."

"The sheriff did a search for any similar finds," she said. "He didn't come up with anything."

"You're thinking a serial killer?"

"They're not as common as they once were but they're still around. My last case in Denver was one. He killed five girls. The youngest was twelve. The oldest was fifteen."

"That must have been a tough case to work."

"They're all tough," she said. "That one was

maybe tougher because I was dating an assistant district attorney at the time and he was putting a lot of pressure on me to come up with identities. We split up shortly after that case was resolved."

There was no mistaking the hurt in her voice, and anger flared. "What a jerk."

She sighed. "He was a jerk. I didn't see it at the time, but he was." She caught his eye. "You're not the only one who was fooled by emotion in a relationship."

"Tell me he didn't steal your car and all your money."

She laughed. "No. He didn't do that. Not that I have any money to steal."

"Neither did I. Not really. I'm sure that was a disappointment to Nora. I hope it was."

Their gazes locked and he felt caught and held by a sudden connection to her, a shared understanding beyond words, as if he could really feel what she was feeling and vice versa. He tried to find his voice, wanting to ask if she was caught this way too, but she looked away and the connection severed, leaving him cold and hollow. He looked away too, pulling himself together. "Is there anything else you'd like to see?" he asked.

"No. We can go."

DANIELLE FOLLOWED CALEB back down the trail. She was glad for the time to try to collect herself. The last thing she expected from this afternoon was to feel so close to him. They had bonded over a shared sense of betrayal, but as heady as that moment of connection felt, she didn't trust emotion anymore. Richard had made her feel all the right things. He had said all the right words, but his actions had proved him a liar and all her emotions false.

Neither of them spoke until they were back at Caleb's truck. "Did you learn anything useful?" he asked.

"Nothing," she said. "But it was good to see the place, at least."

"Would you like to go somewhere and get something to eat?" he asked.

She looked up from fastening her seat belt, then silently cursed herself for not being better at hiding her horror at the idea of anything resembling a date. Now he looked embarrassed. "I just thought you might be hungry," he said.

Suddenly she *was* hungry. Ravenous. "Lunch would be great," she said. There was no danger of falling for Caleb, she reminded herself. He was a man who had sworn off romance. And he was married, no matter how brief and unhappy the union had been.

She agreed that barbecue sounded good, so he drove to a place near the river. The small wooden building sat in the shade of a tall spruce, half a dozen battered wooden picnic tables scattered in front. The scent of smoked meat perfumed the air, and they waited in a line to reach the order window. While they waited, Caleb chatted with two men ahead of them, and introduced them as rock climbers. "Danielle is a scientist," he said. She waited for someone to ask what kind of science, but no one did.

They ordered barbecue sandwiches and found a spot in the shade to eat. "Was that all right, my introducing you as a scientist?" he asked. "I thought it might be awkward, trying to explain why you're really here."

"It is awkward," she said. "People are either horrified or fascinated. The fascinated ones are almost worse, because they want to talk about all the grisly details while we're trying to eat lunch."

He laughed. "Glad to know I saved us from that." He crunched a chip. "How did you end up doing what you do?" he asked. "Putting faces on the dead seems pretty specialized."

"I was an art major in college," she said. "I thought I would use my degree to teach. By my senior year I realized how tough it was going to be to find a job that would allow me to support myself. I attended a career fair at school and someone from a private forensics lab was there. He asked me my major and when I told him art he got excited." She shook her head, remembering the moment with wonder. "That certainly hadn't happened at any of the other tables I had stopped at. He told me about all the positions my degree would be useful in, from crime scene analysis to facial reconstruction. He took out his phone and showed me photos of other reconstructions. I thought it was interesting, but so far from anything I had considered, I admit I blew him off."

She took a long sip of tea, then continued. "But he kept in touch, and he encouraged me to apply for a job. No one else wanted to hire me, so I didn't really have a choice. My parents had died recently and I was on my own. But once I started training in my new job, I discovered I loved it. Every reconstruction involves solving a mystery. Who was this person, and what did they look like? And I got to make a real difference to people—to law enforcement, but most importantly, to the victims' families."

"Butch says you're the best he's ever met at your job and we should count ourselves lucky to have persuaded you to come here," Caleb said.

"Butch is a dear. I worked under his supervision for a while in that first job." She pinched off a piece of her brisket sandwich and popped it in her mouth. She had said enough about herself for now.

Caleb met her gaze and again she felt a warmth spread through her. She quickly looked away. Caleb was a friend, but he couldn't be anything more. She took another bite of the sandwich and was chewing when her phone rang. She groped for it and at the sight of the number felt faint.

"Hey, are you okay?" Caleb leaned across the table. "You've gone white as a ghost."

She swiped down to end the call and laid the phone on the table. "I'm okay." She grabbed for her cup of iced tea and drank deeply.

Caleb stared at the phone as it began ringing again. "Maybe you'd better answer," he said.

She picked up the phone again, though what she really wanted was to hurl it into the woods behind them. "Hello?" She cursed the way her voice shook. Had he heard it?

"Hello, Dani," Richard said. She had let him call her that, even though the first time he used the diminutive she had told him she didn't like it. He had countered that it suited her and she had let it slide. Instance one of a hundred when he had ignored her feelings and she had accepted it. "How are you?"

"What do you want?" she asked, deliberately brusque, aware of Caleb across from her. He was staring toward the barbecue stand, but she had no doubt he was listening to every word of this conversation.

"I want to see you," he said. "I miss you."

I miss you, too. That little voice inside her was a traitor, and she rushed to shove the sentiment down. "I don't miss you," she lied. "Is there anything else? Because I'm going to hang up soon."

"I need your file on Misty Craven," he said.

"You have it. I turned all my files in that case over to your assistant before I left."

"I don't have it. It's probably still in your office. You need to come back and find it for me."

"I don't work for the crime lab anymore, Richard," she said. "If you want the file, go find it yourself." Then she ended the call, the rush of adrenaline that followed leaving her shaking.

Caleb met her gaze, but didn't ask the question. She answered anyway. "That was my ex."

"He wants you back." It was a statement, not a question.

"He's engaged to someone else. And even if he wasn't, I don't want him." Not really.

"That must hurt," he said. "His getting engaged so soon after the two of you split."

"Oh, he got engaged while we were still together." She pushed the remains of her lunch away. "He was dating her at the same time he was dating me. He didn't see any problem about continuing with things the way they were. As long as I kept quiet about our relationship." And agreed not to have his baby.

"Now I really hate him. If I find Nora, maybe you could introduce her to him. It sounds like they would be perfect for each other."

Laughter burst from her, a spring unwound, both startling and joyful. Once she started laughing, she couldn't stop. Caleb joined in, and tears ran down her face. "They would be perfect," she said. "But I doubt Richard would ever fall for her. He likes women he can manipulate."

"Nora would make him think she was like that, until she had reeled him in, then it would be too late."

Danielle dabbed at her eyes with a napkin. "I haven't laughed like that in a long time," she said. "Thanks."

"My pleasure." He smiled and there it was again—that pull inside that started in her chest and went all the way down. A longing for something more.

She missed being with someone. Having a lover. But it worried her that she would never be able to think of any man without suspicion. She didn't want to be that woman. She wanted room in her life for love again, but worried that Richard had ruined her the way Nora had ruined Caleb.

CALEB HAD JUST walked into his apartment after lunch with Danielle when his phone rang. Investigator Dan Phillips's gruff voice got right to the point. "Is there a town near you called Paradise?"

"Yeah. It's about thirty miles from here, on the other side of some mountain passes. Why?"

"Nora was there."

He gripped the phone more tightly. "When?"

"Six weeks ago. She wasn't using the name Nora. She was calling herself Ellie. Ellie Garrison." Elinor Shapiro Garrison. He could see her writing the name in beautiful script on the signature card for their joint bank account. The account she had emptied before she left town.

"You're sure it was her?" he asked.

"The guy I talked to said she was a knockout blonde, about twenty-four. Sounds like the description you gave me. And it was definitely your Ford F-150 she sold at the used car lot in Paradise. Same vehicle identification number. The salesman said she traded it in for a Mustang convertible. He said he'd make you a good deal on the truck if you wanted to buy it back."

No, he didn't want the truck. Not when Nora

had driven it longer than he had. "Did she say where she was going from there?" he asked.

"No. But maybe you should be on the lookout for her."

"She's not here in Eagle Mountain," he said. "The town is too small for her to blend in."

"She's a con artist. People like her are experts at blending in."

Could Nora really be here and he didn't know?

"Do you want me to keep looking for her?" Phillips asked.

"Yes."

"I'll send you a bill." He ended the call and Caleb sagged back against the counter. He wanted to get in his Chevy and drive around town, searching for Nora. And then what? If he confronted her, she would no doubt have some story about what had happened. She would accuse him of overreacting and he would be in danger of walking away, thinking everything was his fault. She had done that before, when he had told her about contacting the American consulate to expedite her passport. "You're just going to confuse things more," she had said, and he had believed her.

Phillips had said she sold the truck six weeks ago. Where had she been since then? He tried to remember if he had seen a Mustang convertible in town. He didn't think so. A car like that stood out. A woman like Nora stood out, too. When she wanted to, she did.

He slammed his hand down on the counter in frustration, welcoming the sting of pain from the hard contact. Looking for Nora in town wouldn't do any good. She wouldn't be found until she was ready to be found. All he could do was wait.

Chapter Seven

Danielle studied the woman's face taking shape beneath her fingers. In the past few days, she had affixed all the markers at the appropriate depths, as dictated by the computer program she used. Then she had filled in between the markers with strips of clay and smoothed them. Already the figure was looking more like a human head and less like a Halloween decoration. But now the real artistry began as she worked to sculpt the nose. The nose was such a prominent feature on a person's face that getting it wrong could ruin the whole reconstruction. No one would recognize the woman if her nose wasn't right.

But soft tissue was the first to decay, leaving behind few clues as to what the woman's nose had really been like. Danielle did have a few places she could look for clues. She considered the upper portion of the nasal opening. Recent research had shown that the shape of the tip of the nose mimicked this shape. In this case, the nasal opening was narrow and pointed, so Danielle would sculpt the nose to have a narrow pointed tip. In order to determine how far the nose protruded, she took measurements at various points around the nasal opening and plugged these into a computer program. The program used these measurements to determine angles where the points intersected. The resulting image showed how wide the nose was and how far it protruded.

These formulas weren't foolproof. If someone had had surgery to reshape their nose, or an injury that affected the nose, the reconstruction wouldn't match reality. But in most cases the math enabled reconstructionists to come close to giving their subjects features that closely matched those the person had had in life.

But math couldn't smooth the contours and flare the nostrils in a way that looked *right* with the rest of the face. That was up to Danielle. She began shaping the clay with her hands and small tools, carving away here and adding there. Gradually the woman's nose took shape, and with it the rest of her face. Cheeks looked more like cheeks when attached to a nose, and the eyes looked more lifelike when looking out over something besides a vacant hole.

When she was done, Danielle's neck and

shoulders and lower back ached from bending over the worktable. But Jane Doe now had a long narrow nose, very slightly upturned at the tip. Danielle would need to work more on the brow and eyelids to give the woman expression, but that would have to wait. Tomorrow she would create the lips. They would be narrow too, the lower lip a bit more prominent, judging by the jaw structure. Part of her wanted to get right to work completing the face but she knew better than to continue when she was tired. All she would do was end up wasting materials.

She stood and stretched, then looked out the window. Butch was in his front yard, staring at something in the grass. She needed to keep her promise to herself to talk to him, and now was as good a time as any.

He stood as she approached. "Hello, Danielle," he said. "How are things with you?"

"Good. I just finished the nose."

"You're making good progress, then?"

"Yes. What were you looking at?" She nodded toward the ground where he had been crouched.

"A grasshopper. I was wondering if it would make good bait."

She laughed. "Do you ever think about anything but fishing?"

"In the fall, I think about hunting. And fishing."

"What do you do in the winter?"

"Ice fish, of course." He smiled. "Are you getting out and seeing any of this beautiful country, or are you spending all your time in your workroom?"

"I was up at the Silverpeak Mine yesterday," she said.

"Oh? You went up there by yourself?"

The glint in his eye told her he knew that wasn't the case. "Caleb Garrison took me," she said.

"Caleb is an interesting man," Butch said.

Did Butch have any idea what Caleb had been through? Danielle doubted it. Caleb had talked as if he had kept his story secret, only telling her because he was desperate to know if her Jane Doe was Nora. "How well do you know him?" she asked.

"He and I have had several discussions about local history. And I've seen him on several search and rescue calls. It takes a special person to put in that kind of effort for others."

"Yes." She admired Caleb for that. Many people, crushed by the kind of betrayal he had experienced, would have retreated from the world. That was what she had wanted to do— what she had done, in leaving her job and grabbing onto Butch's invitation to come here.

But Caleb hadn't retreated. Instead he had

chosen to devote time and energy to helping others. "I never told you what happened in Denver," she said. "Why I broke down at that press conference, and why I quit my job."

"I could see you were hurting," he said. "But I didn't think it was my business to pry."

"You're not like most people, then." She made a face. "My coworkers were so concerned about me, but I could see in their eyes that they just wanted the latest gossip."

"You seem better now," he said. "That's what's most important."

"I am." She tucked her arm in his. "Let's sit down and talk."

They walked together to a pair of patio chairs on his front porch. "You remember me talking about Richard?" she asked. "The assistant DA I was seeing?"

"Yes." Butch's expression was solemn. "He was at that press conference, too. I noticed he never looked at you, not even when you broke down."

She remembered that, and how much his snub had wounded her. "I thought I loved him. I thought he was the man I would spend the rest of my life with. Then I found out I was pregnant. I was scared, and then I was elated. I thought he would be, too."

Butch said nothing. He was one of those rare

people with a gift for silence. Danielle gripped the arms of the chair, then forced her fingers to relax. "Richard was not happy. He told me he didn't want children, and that I would have to end the pregnancy. I pushed back. I told him I wanted this baby. Then I found out he didn't want me." She rested her hand on her belly.

"I wondered," Butch said.

"You did?" She stared at him.

He smiled. "I've known you a long time. I could see there was something different. And I may be an old bachelor, but I'm still a doctor. Now go on with your story. Richard dumped you."

"He got engaged to the mayor's daughter. A very politically advantageous match. It turns out he had been dating her at the same time he was seeing me."

"Is he the reason you left your job with the Denver Crime Lab?"

"Yes. I knew I was going to keep the baby and I didn't want to deal with the gossip. And after that press conference when I broke down on camera…" She pressed a tissue to her eyes, fighting to keep back fresh tears.

"You shouldn't have to apologize for honest emotion," Butch said.

"I shouldn't have to, but you know how it is. At work we're all supposed to be calm, hardworking automatons. Men are tough and women are supposed to be even tougher. Emotions are too messy and other people—especially men like Richard—don't want to deal with them."

"I'm sorry you felt you had to leave a job you loved."

"Richard tried to get me to stay. The way he saw it, I would terminate the pregnancy, he would marry Jenna and he'd keep seeing me on the side. Everything would be perfect. Perfect for him, anyway. He explained all this to me as if it made all the sense in the world. I was so angry with him I taunted him. I told him I would stay in my job, but that I'd have the baby and I'd make sure everyone knew he was the father. That was a big mistake. He threatened me."

Butch sat up straighter. "You should have reported him."

She shook her head. "I couldn't. He said he would tell everyone about my breakdown, that I had been confined to a psychiatric hospital for treatment."

"You entered the hospital voluntarily," Butch said. "Because you knew it was the right thing to do."

"That doesn't matter." She leaned toward him. "I know I'm supposed to speak up against that kind of manipulation and take him to court for discrimination or something, but I can't go through all that. I can't have my past dragged through the courts and the papers. Especially when Richard threatened to use my history against me when it came to the baby. He said he would sue for custody and any judge would agree that I was an unfit mother."

"That isn't true," Butch said.

"It doesn't matter if it's true. As an assistant district attorney, Richard knows everyone in the court system. He's charming and well liked. He's good friends with a lot of judges. It's easy to believe he wouldn't have any trouble finding one who would side with him in a custody battle."

"But he told you he didn't want children."

"He doesn't. But I believe he would fight for custody to get back at me. One of the reasons he's such a good prosecutor is that he can't stand to lose. He'll go to great lengths to avoid losing."

"I'm sorry you had to go through all of that," Butch said. "But I'm glad you felt comfortable confiding in me."

"I haven't told anyone else." She smoothed her T-shirt over her belly again. "Though I suppose I'll have to soon."

"You don't have to make an announcement,"

Butch said. "Let people figure it out for themselves."

"I don't know, Butch. I'm living here—maybe people will think the baby is yours."

He laughed, a loud guffaw. "Then let them. At my age, it would probably enhance my reputation." His expression sobered. "But seriously, I think you're handling all of this very well. If there's anything I can do to help, just say the word."

"You've already done so much." She looked up at the top of a blue spruce, the lacy fronds the color of stormy seas. "Coming here was a good idea. And getting back to work helped more than I would have thought it could."

"We really did need you," Butch said. "I'm glad the timing worked out."

"I was going to take a walk," she said. "Will you come with me?"

"All right."

They headed down the street at an easy pace. They had reached the end when a Honda sedan turned the corner and drove slowly past them. Danielle recognized the couple who lived at the first house on the left. The man was driving, and glared at them as he passed, while the woman, Carissa, smiled and waved. The car turned into the drive, pulled into the garage and the door slid closed behind them. "Do you know them?" Danielle asked.

"I believe their name is Miller," Butch said. "But I've never met them."

"I met Carissa out walking one day. She's expecting a baby too, in September. She seemed very nice."

"I'm glad you're making friends here," he said. "And you're welcome to stay here as long as you like. You could stay until your baby is born, or after."

"And what am I going to do for work?" she asked.

"You could offer your services as a freelancer," he said. "I already told you we don't have any forensic reconstructionists on this side of the state, and the labs in Denver and Salt Lake City are constantly running behind. Your reputation would guarantee you would have all the work you could handle. And you could work here, where you could keep an eye on the baby."

He painted a picture of such a rosy future, but she was skeptical. "I don't know, Butch. It sounds too good to be true."

"You don't have to decide anything right away, but think about it."

"I will."

They turned and started back down the

street. They hadn't gone far before Butch's phone sounded. He pulled it from his pocket. "I'm sorry, I have to go," he said.

"Is something wrong?"

"I have to put on my coroner's hat," he said. "A drowning."

"I'm sorry."

He pocketed the phone. "Sorry for the family, yes. The message said Search and Rescue is on scene. If I see Caleb, I'll tell him you said hello."

"Butch, you aren't playing matchmaker, are you?" she asked, amused. "Because neither Caleb nor I are interested."

"You must be imagining things," he said. "Now I'd better leave you."

He jogged toward his house, surprisingly fast for a man his size and age, she mused.

Then her thoughts turned back to Caleb. Had he had to pull a dead body from a river or lake? Were there survivors he needed to tend to? She wanted to call him later and ask, but she would wait until Jane Doe was ready for him to view. By now she was almost as curious as he was to know if Jane Doe was Nora.

THE CALL CAME in at 1:17 that afternoon. A family in an inflatable raft on Grizzly Creek had overturned and were stranded in the water. At least two people were missing. Bystanders were trying to help.

"We'll be lucky if we don't have to rescue the bystanders, too," Sheri said as they packed gear at SAR headquarters. "People go in to help and they end up in trouble or drowned." She looked over her shoulder. "Be sure you've got plenty of PFDs and extra helmets."

Loaded up, they drove as far as they were able, then parked, unloaded gear and hiked up the riverbank. Normally Grizzly Creek was a shallow, though swift-running, waterway with too many exposed boulders and snags to make it navigable. But heavy snowmelt had raised the water level enough to make it tempting for boaters. Half a dozen people were on the banks, two up to their waists in midstream.

A man in fishing waders hurried to meet them. "I was on the bank, getting ready to leave, when I saw it happen," he said. "The raft caught on a snag and upended. It tipped everyone into the water."

"How many people?" Sheri asked.

"Five. Mom and Dad and three children— little kids." He turned and pointed. "One of the boys is trapped on the snag and his brother is over near the opposite bank, hanging onto that tree. We've been trying to reach them, but the current is so strong."

"You did the right thing, calling for help," Sheri said. "We'll take over now."

The first boy was all the way out of the water, balanced precariously amid the roots of a dead tree that had been dragged down the river to lodge in this bend. The family's raft, blue and partially deflated, was pressed up against the trunk of the tree. The boy's face was very pale above his blue life jacket, his mouth open as if screaming, but the roar of the water drowned out his voice.

The other boy, who looked smaller to Caleb, had only his head out of the water, clinging to another downed tree, the current pulling at him. As the SAR team moved closer to the water, a clot of spectators parted to reveal a woman seated in the mud beside the water, her hair wet and snarled, her clothing soaked. She tried to rise, but fell back, and another woman helped her up again. "My boys," she said. "Please save my boys." Then she began to sob, and the other woman pulled her close.

"A couple of guys were able to pull her out," the woman holding the distraught mother said. "One of them went back in to get the kids, but he was swept away."

"Where is the father?" Sheri asked. "And there's another child?"

"The current dragged them downriver," another man said. "It all happened so fast."

"Caleb, you, Grace and Danny grab throw lines and head downstream," Sheri directed. "Look for the missing men and the child. Eldon, you and Carrie, Tony, Ryan and I will string a line to the child in the water."

Caleb and the others headed toward the Beast to retrieve the weighted lines they could toss to anyone in the water. On the way, they passed two men and a woman with clipboards, all three wearing dark sunglasses. "Who are they?" Caleb asked.

"I think they're the observers from the Mountain Rescue Association," Danny said.

"They look like they're from the FBI," Grace said.

"Never mind them," Danny said. "Let's get moving." They grabbed the lines, then jogged down the bank, searching the water for any flash of color that might mean a person caught in the current. The accident had happened at least half an hour before. Though no one said anything, they all knew the odds weren't on their side of finding any of the three alive. The strong current could easily pull a person under, and the many snags and boulders could batter a person to death, if they didn't succumb to the icy temperatures. Still, one of the missing might have climbed onto a snag or boulder, like the first boy, or be clinging to life like the second.

They hadn't gone far before a man approached them. He was soaked through, his T-shirt almost torn from his body, his legs streaked with blood. Danny and Caleb rushed to steady him. "Were you in the raft that capsized?" Danny asked.

The man nodded. "One minute we were fine, having fun. The next, we were in the water. I lay on my back and floated with the current until I came to a place that was shallow enough to stand."

"You're bleeding," Danny said. He knelt and examined the man's legs. "Looks like you got cut up pretty bad on the rocks."

The man looked down. "I didn't even realize."

Shock and cold water had probably numbed the man to the pain. "Where's your life jacket?" Caleb asked.

"My wife and I are good swimmers," the man said. "We didn't have jackets. But we made the kids wear them. We made sure of that. And the two older boys are good swimmers. The youngest, Casey, he hasn't had lessons yet." His voice broke. "I couldn't find him," he said. "He was there in the water right by me, but before I could grab him, he was gone."

Danny straightened. "We're going to look for your son," he said. "Grace is going to take you back to your wife."

"Come on." Grace moved in to put her arm around the man. "Walk with me. I'll take you to your wife and your other two boys."

"Are they all right?" he asked.

But Caleb never heard the answer as he and Danny hurried downstream. His stomach was in knots now, thinking of a little boy in that frigid roiling water.

"I see something." Danny stopped and pointed.

At first Caleb didn't see anything but water and rocks. Then he spotted it—a flash of red amid the white foam. They moved closer. Soon he could make out the legs and lower torso of a man, clad in red swim trunks. The rest of him was submerged in a tangle of brush commonly referred to as a strainer, because it acted like a sieve to catch larger pieces of debris. Danny called on his radio. "We've found a man's body," he said. "About a quarter mile down from the accident site, caught in a strainer, about ten feet out from the bank."

"We'll send a team down," Sheri said.

"Grace and the dad are headed your way,"

Danny said. "Dad got banged up on the rocks, but he's okay."

"The first boy is out. We've got a chopper on the way to transport him to the children's hospital," Sheri said. "We've got a line to the other boy and should have him ashore soon. Any sign of the youngest boy?"

"Not yet."

They spent some time exploring the strainer, since it was a likely place for a body to wash up. From the bank, they were able to reach several branches, which they hauled to shore, in case the boy had become trapped underneath. They had hauled the last of these out of the way when Danny straightened. "I don't think the kid is in there," he said. "Let's look farther downstream."

Other SAR members, as well as sheriff's department deputies and others who had been on the river were also searching. Cries of "Casey!" echoed up and down the river. As the minutes stretched toward over an hour, Caleb's spirits sank. Even if they found the boy now, he wouldn't be alive.

"I see something in the water!" the woman's scream reached them from where she stood on the bank. Caleb and Danny ran to her, along with several others. "Down there!" She pointed to an undercut in the bank. Caleb recognized the bright yellow of a life jacket, a shock of wet blond hair floated above it. The boy was face-down in the water.

"Come on." Danny slapped Caleb's back, then half slid down the steep bank. The water was calm and shallow where the boy had landed, cut off from the main channel by a massive cottonwood log that formed a natural dam. The two men waded in. Mud sucked at Caleb's boots, and the water was icy, though coming up only to his knees. "Get on his other side," Danny directed. "I think this life jacket is caught on something. Do you have a knife?"

Caleb unclipped the pocketknife that was part of his rescue gear and handed it to Danny, who plunged one hand into the water and be-neath the boy. "Hold onto him," Danny di-rected. "Don't let him drift away."

Caleb bent and grabbed hold of the boy's arm. It felt icy, but maybe that was only the re-sult of being submerged in the cold river. With a grunt, Danny sliced through whatever had been holding the boy fast. He returned Caleb's knife, and together they lifted the small child's body out of the water.

"Don't turn him over yet," Danny said, when Caleb started to do so. Instead he took the child and held him over one arm, facedown, and gave him two sharp slaps on the back. Then he put his fingers in Casey's mouth and pulled out a wad of leaves and mud. He slapped him again, and a little water dribbled out.

Sheri and Hannah met them on the bank. Deputies moved the crowd out of the way and Danny laid the little boy on his side in the grass. Caleb stared at the still, white face. "Here's the AED," Sheri said, and handed Hannah the red plastic box containing the automated electronic defibrillator.

"Why are they bothering?" someone behind Caleb muttered. "The kid's been in there over an hour."

Caleb had been wondering the same thing, but he forced his thoughts to the procedure in front of him. Though he had practiced using the AED on a dummy in class, he had never needed to unpack one in a real life-and-death situation. Hannah flipped a switch and began placing the electrodes before the electronic voice even began instructing her. The machine was designed so that even someone without experience could use it, simply by doing everything the electronic voice instructed. Seconds later Hannah announced "Clear!" and the little boy's body convulsed as the shock jolted through him. Hannah stopped, placed the end of her stethoscope to the boy's chest and listened, then looked to Danny.

"Again," Danny said.

They shocked the boy twice more before Hannah lifted the stethoscope off Casey's chest. She spoke so softly only those standing very close could hear. "I've got a heartbeat," she said. "It's faint, but it's there."

"Get that litter over here!" Danny shouted.

Caleb and Sheri moved in with the litter. They transferred the body, then they, along with Hannah and Danny, grabbed the four corners. "Run!" Sheri ordered, and they raced toward the road and the waiting medical helicopter.

Caleb had little memory afterward of that desperate run over rough ground. From time to time one of them stumbled, but the others kept the litter steady, the pale small figure in it so still and silent. By the time they reached the waiting helicopter, Caleb's hand ached from gripping the stretcher and blood ran down one knee from where he had fallen on the rocks. They passed the boy off to the medical flight crew, then melted back into the crowd to watch as the chopper lifted into a sky that was already graying with dusk.

"He's got a chance now," Sheri said, as the helicopter rose over the ridge and disappeared from view.

"How is that even possible?" Caleb asked. "He must have been in the water over an hour."

"Children can go into a sort of suspended animation in cold water like that," Danny said.

"It's called the diving response," Hannah said. "Researchers think it's triggered by a sudden drop in body temperature. If they can keep his heart beating and gradually warm his body, he may be okay."

"Let's hope so," Sheri said.

Caleb looked around at the dispersing crowd. "Where is his family?" he asked.

"They went to the hospital to be with their other two children," Sheri said. "Hopefully, they'll have good news about their youngest boy when they get there."

"How are the other boys?" Danny asked.

"The oldest is fine," Sheri said. "Scared and cold, but unharmed. The middle son is in serious condition, but with a good chance of survival."

They all fell silent as they neared the figure of Butch Collins, who was kneeling beside the body they had retrieved from the river earlier. Butch stood at their approach. "He's ready for you to take him to the waiting vehicle," he said.

"Do we know who he is?" Sheri asked.

"The friend who was with him identified him as Liam Marshall," Butch said. "He helped pull the mom out of the water, then went back to try to help the kids and got caught in the current."

"Where is his friend now?" Caleb asked.

"He went to call Liam's family."

Hannah moved in to cover the man's face and the others prepared to lift the litter. The dead man was much heavier than the child had been, and there was no haste in walking him down the road to the waiting mortuary vehicle. Butch fell into step alongside Caleb. "Tough day," Butch said.

Caleb nodded. "I hope the little boy makes it," he said.

"We all do." Sheri spoke from the other side of the litter. "But no matter what happens, remember that we saved his two brothers, and kept bystanders who weren't trained from going in after them. More lives would have been lost without us here. You have to remember that."

"I'll remember," Caleb said. They dropped off the body, collected the empty litter and returned to the riverbank, where he helped to coil ropes and gather equipment. It was full dark by the time he returned to his vehicle, his limbs leaden, footsteps dragging.

He was startled when a man stepped out to meet him. Shock turned to curiosity when he recognized Butch Collins. Why had the coroner waited for him all this time? "Danielle tells me you took her up to Silverpeak Mine," Butch said.

"I don't think it told her anything new about her victim, but it was a beautiful hike," Caleb said.

"She's had a tough time of it," Butch said.

So that was what this was about—Butch was feeling protective of his friend. As if she had anything to fear from Caleb. "She told me a little of what happened, with that jerk she was involved with," he said. "You don't have to worry about me. We're just friends."

"She could use friends now." Butch shoved his hands into the pockets of his baggy trousers. "Someone closer to her own age."

"You make it sound like you're ancient."

"I'm old enough to be your father, and that makes me feel ancient."

Caleb realized he didn't know that much about the coroner—whether he had ever been married, or if he had children somewhere. "How do you know Danielle?" he asked.

"She was my trainee, years ago, when I worked for a forensics lab in Denver. When she was just out of college, a wonderful girl, already showing signs of her brilliant talent."

"She's lucky to have a friend like you," Caleb said.

Butch pulled his keys from his pocket. "She thinks I'm matchmaking."

With me? The idea startled Caleb, but maybe not as much as it should have. Under other circumstances, he might have pursued Danielle. She was beautiful and smart and he liked being with her. "Are you?" he asked after an awkward pause.

Butch's gaze met his. "I don't believe in matchmaking," he said. "I think romance is a strictly do-it-yourself proposition." He nodded and walked away, to his own car.

Right. Well, so far Caleb had been a failure at DIY romance, considering his disaster of a marriage.

He met up with the rest of the team back at SAR headquarters. "Mo's sent over pizza," Sheri said. "And a card that says thank you for all your efforts. And I just heard from Casey's dad. Casey is awake and talking. Apparently, he survived his ordeal unscathed. His brother Carter is doing better, too."

A cheer rose and the mood in the room lifted. Caleb sat at the long table with the others and dug in, and began to feel better. They talked about everything but rescue work—construction being done on new mountain biking trails, the lineup of bands for a series of concerts in the park that summer, and all the gossip about who was hooking up with whom and who had moved where or who had acquired some coveted new possession. "Did you see the tricked-out Jeep the mayor is driving these days?" Ryan asked.

"I saw it," Tony said. "LED light bars, lifted suspension, those big knobby tires. He can go anywhere in that monster."

"That's great for the trails, but not a smooth ride on the highway," Sheri said.

"So if you came into a bunch of money, what would be your dream ride?" Ryan asked.

"A Mustang convertible," she said, without hesitation. "Not exactly practical here in the mountains, but I'd love it for cruising around in the summer."

"I saw one of those in Junction last week," Danny said as he helped himself to another slice of pizza. "This cute blonde was behind the wheel. She saw me staring and blew a kiss before she raced off."

The pizza Caleb had eaten felt like rocks in his stomach. He stared at his plate, willing himself not to be sick.

"Caleb, are you okay?" Carrie asked.

"Sure. I'm fine." He pushed back his chair and stood. "Something just went down the wrong way."

There were lots of cute blonde women in the world, he reminded himself once he was in the privacy of the bathroom. And some of them probably owned Mustang convertibles. That didn't mean the woman Danny saw was Nora. Though blowing that kiss was the kind of thing she would do. She was a skilled flirt—flirting was how she had reeled him in.

All he wanted now was for her to let him go.

Chapter Eight

A week after she was pulled from Silverpeak Mine, Jane Doe had a face. Danielle had transformed the discarded skull into the head of a woman—a young woman, pleasant-looking, though not strikingly beautiful. She had a long face with well-defined cheekbones, a narrow nose and lips and a slightly pointed chin. Danielle had given her a light brown wig of shoulder-length hair, bangs swept to one side across her high forehead. She stared out at the world with one brow slightly raised, as if questioning all that lay before her.

"I wanted you to be the first to see her," she told Caleb, as she led him over to the worktable. She had arranged a scarf around the woman's neck, so that she looked less like a disembodied head and more like someone standing behind the worktable. "I think she came out very well. I can't be sure about the eye and hair color, but I think the rest is accurate, judging by her bone structure. It's hard to be definite, but…" She pressed her lips together, aware that she was babbling.

Caleb was staring, not saying anything, his expression impossible to read. He walked all the way around the table, studying the head as if trying to memorize the features. Danielle was getting nervous. Maybe she had made a mistake, revealing this to him first.

He stopped and turned from the head to her. "It's not Nora," he said.

The intensity of her relief startled her. Why? If it had been Caleb's ex-wife, would that have meant he could have been involved in her death? She dismissed the idea. "That's good, right?"

"Yes, it's good, of course." He turned back to the head, lines on his forehead deeper. "She looks familiar, though."

Goose bumps formed on her arms and she rubbed them absently. "Do you think you might know her?"

"Not really. Just…maybe I've seen her around town. Or on campus?"

Danielle moved closer and readjusted the scarf. "I'm going to take her to the sheriff's department this afternoon," she said. "They'll photograph her and distribute the photo to the media. If she's local, someone will recognize her."

"It's an eerie feeling, thinking I might know her," he said. "That means I might know her killer, too."

Danielle laid her hand on the back of the head. "So she isn't anything like Nora? Not even if I had chosen a blond wig?"

"No. Nora's face was rounder. Her eyes were farther apart and she had a dimple on the right side of her mouth."

He spoke with the certainty of someone who knew another's features intimately. Which, of course, he did. "Are you disappointed that you don't know where she is?"

He sighed. "The investigator I hired says she's close."

"Really? How close?"

"She sold my truck to a used car dealer in Paradise six weeks ago," he said. "She traded it in for a Mustang convertible. Previously, she told a coworker in Denver that she was going to look for me and Paradise is definitely close to here."

"What's she been doing for the past six weeks?" Danielle asked.

"Who knows?" He blew out another breath. "Last week one of the other Search and Rescue volunteers said a blonde in a Mustang convertible flirted with him at a traffic light in Junction. That doesn't mean it was her, but what if it was?"

"You can serve her with the divorce papers," Danielle said.

"I could." But he didn't look happy, or even relieved. In fact he looked miserable.

She moved closer to him. "What's wrong?" she asked softly.

His eyes met hers, and she read her own struggle in there. "Maybe I'm a coward, but I'm a little afraid of her," he said. "Afraid of the power she has over me. She completely took me in before, and it happened so fast. I don't trust her, and I don't trust my own judgment when it comes to her."

She nodded. "I feel that way about my ex," she said. "At least a little bit. Richard didn't deliberately scam me, but he was very good at telling me what I wanted to hear. When I was with him, his charm deceived me to the kind of person he really was. That makes me doubt myself. I used to think I was a good judge of people before him."

"Yeah. Me, too." Some of the bleakness went out of his expression. "And whatever happens with Nora, I'm not going to fall for her again. She stole from me, not just my money and my truck, but my dignity. She'll probably try to charm me, but I have to be impervious by now, right?"

"I don't think you're a coward." She patted his arm, his biceps hard beneath her palm. His gaze met hers again and something flared there, heat and intensity. She tried to take a steadying breath, but only inhaled his scent of warm cotton and clean skin.

He leaned closer, and the tips of her breasts brushed against his chest. "Danielle," he whispered.

She tilted her head up to him, lips slightly parted. "Caleb," she said, and then before she lost her nerve, she pressed her lips to his.

His arms tightened around her, pulling the length of her against him, and his lips caressed hers, firing sensation everywhere he touched. Her fingers dug into his biceps. These weren't the arms of a coward. These were arms that could carry a child to safety or haul a fellow volunteer up a mountain slope. Strong arms that could protect those he loved, yet tender enough to cherish also.

She wanted to cherish and protect, too. She wanted to believe the heartache she had suffered was something she could come back from, only stronger. Kissing him now, she felt invincible.

He broke the kiss and stared down at her.

"Maybe we shouldn't have done that," he said, his voice husky.

She blinked, and something like terror washed over her. What was she doing? The very last thing she needed in her life right now was a man. Especially a married man with an unpredictable, possibly criminal, wife. She pushed away from him and stepped back. "No. We shouldn't have done that. I'm sorry."

"I'd better go now," he said.

She nodded. "Yes. You'd better." What had possessed her to kiss him that way? Nothing good came of impulses like that.

She waited until he had driven away before she looked at the head of the mystery woman. She was glad this wasn't Nora. She didn't want to have that between her and Caleb. But her goal was always to restore the identities of the victims entrusted to her care. "Who are you?" she asked the silent staring face, as she had so many times before. "What happened to you?" And what had happened to Danielle herself, that her life had taken such an unexpected turn?

THE PHOTOGRAPH OF the unknown woman filled one-quarter of the front page of the next issue of the *Eagle Mountain Examiner*. Speculation about her identity was a chief topic of conversation at the coffee shop and the bars, among friends and coworkers. Someone left a copy of the paper on the table at Search and Rescue headquarters, and volunteers gathered around it at the group's regular meeting.

"It's spooky how she looks so alive," Eldon said as he frowned down at the image. The sculpted head had been photographed close-up, looking solemnly into the camera. Her expression, lips together, one eyebrow lifted slightly, suggested she was skeptical about the photographer's—and the viewer's—motives. A second photo on page three showed the image in profile.

Danny leaned over Eldon's shoulder to study the paper. "She looks familiar," he said.

"I thought so, too," Sheri agreed. "But I can't decide if it's because I've really seen her, or because she's so ordinary. Average-looking, I mean. She isn't strikingly beautiful, and she doesn't have really unusual features. She's the type of person who doesn't really stand out."

"Maybe you're right," Danny said. "I can't say I'm that good about paying attention to people's faces. In my job and on a rescue, I'm more focused on their injuries and their medical needs."

"We don't really see people at their best," Carrie said. She studied the photo also. "I can tell you about the injuries of people we rescued, but I couldn't describe the appearance of many of them to you."

"Sure you could," Ryan said. "You could say he was a big guy with blood running down his face from the gash on his forehead. Or, she was a woman with muscular calves who tore a tendon in her knee in a climbing fall."

Carrie swatted at him. "That wouldn't be very helpful in identifying someone years later."

"If she was from around here, someone would have reported her missing," Tony said. "The sheriff said there isn't anyone like this woman in their records."

"So she came from somewhere else," Carrie said. "Was she a tourist?"

"Or was she killed somewhere else and brought here?" Eldon asked.

"We can speculate all day," Sheri said. "But that isn't doing us or her any good. Let's get this meeting underway so we're not here all night."

The first item on the agenda was the Mountain Rescue Association Certification. "They've looked at our records and observed on that river rescue last week," Sheri said. "I understand they've interviewed a few of you?"

"They asked me some questions," Grace said. "The guy told me I gave the right answers."

"They had me explain the rigging we'd use for a canyon rescue," Ryan said. "They had me draw a diagram and label everything. It felt like a test in school, but they seemed okay with what I gave them."

"I know it's stressful," Sheri said. "But it's important. Keep up the good work."

Talk moved on to upcoming training opportunities, other volunteer opportunities in the community and items for the next meeting. "That's everything," Sheri finally said. "See you at the next meeting, or the next callout, whichever comes first."

Chairs shoved back and voices rose in conversation. Caleb slid the newspaper over to study the photo of Jane Doe once more. Seeing her in Danielle's studio had been unsettling, the disembodied head staring at him.

His emotions had been in such turmoil that afternoon—relief that the dead woman wasn't Nora, then despair when he realized his ex was still on the loose, possibly plotting to upset his life in some way again. Then Danielle had kissed him. Obviously the two of them were physically attracted to each other, but he had been doing his best to ignore those feelings and keep things friendly. But when her lips touched his, he hadn't just wanted that kiss, he had needed it. And he hadn't wanted to stop with kissing.

Which was one more reason to pull back. His passion for Nora had been intense, too. And his lust had clouded him to everything that was wrong about their relationship—to all he didn't know about her, all he never bothered to question. He wasn't going to make that mistake again.

He studied the newspaper photos of the woman from the mine. Sheri was right—she was an ordinary woman. Nothing about her stood out.

"What do you think?" Grace stood at his elbow.

"She looks familiar to me," Caleb said. "But I can't think where I would know her from." He slid the paper away. "Maybe I just want to know her. I brought her out of that mine shaft, and part of me wants the closure of knowing who she was and how she got there."

"Her poor family," Grace said. "Surely they've been missing her."

"Maybe she ran away. Or she was hiding from someone," Caleb said.

"You mean, she didn't want to be found?" Grace looked puzzled.

Caleb shrugged. "It happens. Her family might not even know she's dead." Nora had certainly done a good job of hiding from him all these months. If she had died, he wouldn't have known it. She had told him her family was all dead. The thought of her, alone in the world, had made him want to protect her that much more. And then she had told him she was pregnant and that had set the hook and allowed her to reel him in. Part of the pain of discovering she had lied about everything had been grieving the death of his dream of being a father.

He glanced at the photo again. Jane Doe didn't look anything like Nora, but she was another woman with secrets. Would learning her identity lead to her killer or only a bigger puzzle?

FRIDAY AFTER JANE DOE'S picture was released to the media, Butch knocked on Danielle's door and handed her two business cards. "The first is the sheriff in Mesa County. He has a John Doe found in a field near I-70 several months ago. He's been waiting to get on the schedule with a reconstructionist in Denver." He smirked. "It seems they're shorthanded since one of their staff members departed. I told him I knew someone who might be able to help and I'd ask you to give him a call."

She studied the card. "You really are determined to keep me here, aren't you?" she asked.

"Do you want to go back to Denver?"

She shook her head. The longer she stayed in the peace and beauty of this place, the more reluctant she was to leave. Part of that was probably because the people here didn't know her. They didn't know about her past mistakes and didn't have any reason to judge her. But she needed to earn a living, and working on the Jane Doe from the mine had reminded her how much she enjoyed her work. "I'll give him a call." She shuffled to the second card.

"That's for an ob-gyn in Junction," Butch said. "She comes highly recommended."

Danielle glanced down. Though she wore a loose top, she was aware of a slight swell beneath it. Would others notice? "Should I tell her you referred me?" she asked.

"Better not," he said. "She and I dated a few years back and it didn't end well. She accused me of liking fish more than I liked her."

Danielle laughed. "And did you?"

"Let's just say it was a close call when it came to how I wanted to spend my time, but she is definitely a far better physician than any trout I ever met."

"I'll keep that in mind." She tucked the cards in her pocket. "Thank you, Butch. But if I'm going to stay here, I need to start paying you rent."

"I'm sure we can come to some agreement." He checked his watch. "I have to go now. I have a date with a trout."

Laughing, she started to close the door, but stopped when someone called her name. Butch was halfway to his SUV and he stopped to look also as Carissa Miller walked up the driveway. "I was taking my walk and thought I'd stop and say hello," Carissa said. "This isn't a bad time, is it?"

"No. Come on in." Danielle waited while Carissa puffed her way up the steps.

"Make way for the pregnant lady," Carissa said. "I already feel like a walrus and I'm only twenty-one weeks. By the time this baby is born I'll have to wheel my belly around on a cart in front of me."

"You're not as big as all that," Danielle said. She held the door wide and Carissa came in.

"Oh, this is cute," Carissa said, looking around the small apartment. "How did you luck into this?"

"I've known Butch for years," Danielle said. "Have a seat and I'll get us both some water."

"Water would be great. These days, if I'm not hungry, I'm thirsty. Or sleepy." She settled onto the sofa, and fit a pillow behind her back. "So, how did you end up in Eagle Mountain? We're not exactly on everyone's radar."

"I came out here to do some work." Danielle returned with two glasses of iced water and handed one to Carissa. "Butch offered to let me stay here. I'm thinking about renting the place from him on a longer-term basis."

Carissa sipped the water. "What kind of work do you do?" she asked.

"I'm a forensic reconstructionist," Danielle said. "I did the reconstruction of the face of the woman who was featured in the paper yesterday."

"That skeleton they found up at that old mine?" Carissa leaned forward, all avid interest. "I saw the pictures in the paper. You did that?"

"I did," Danielle said.

"From just a skull, right? I think I saw a show about that on TV once."

"That's right."

"Now that's a job you don't come across every day." Carissa sat back. "And you're thinking of sticking around here?"

"I am." She had made a decision—not a sudden impulse, because she had been thinking for a while that she needed to let more people know about her baby. "I'm going to have a baby and I think Eagle Mountain might be a good place to raise a child."

"You're preggers, too!" Carissa shoved up off

the sofa and enveloped Danielle in a hug. "Congratulations." She stepped back and looked Danielle up and down. "Now that you mention it, I do see it. Not that most people would guess. How are you feeling?"

"Good," Danielle said. "A little tired sometimes. Hungry sometimes. And I get out of breath."

Carissa was nodding. "What about your sense of smell? Are you like a bloodhound, all these smells just coming at you?"

"Yes." Just this morning she had thrown out an onion that had overwhelmed her every time she walked into the kitchen.

"I'm so excited," Carissa said. "It will be so fun to know someone else who is going through all this, and when our babies are born, they'll be only a few months apart. When are you due?"

"November 14."

"And you're doing this by yourself?" She held up a hand. "You don't have to answer that if you don't want to. Joey always says I'm too nosy."

"The baby's father isn't interested in being involved," Danielle said.

Carissa nodded. "There's a whole story behind those words, I'll bet, but you don't have to tell me," she said. "You're obviously a smart, strong woman. I mean, if you can mess around with dead people's bones, changing dirty diapers shouldn't even make you blink."

Danielle laughed at this comparison, one she never would have made herself. But she appreciated Carissa's vote of confidence, however it was phrased. "Thanks," she said. "Part of me is terrified of having a baby."

"It is terrifying," Carissa agreed, though she didn't sound afraid. "How do you raise a kid without totally screwing it up?"

"I hadn't even gotten that far," Danielle said. "I'm still trying to figure out where to put a crib and if I'm taking the right vitamins."

"One thing for sure, these babies are coming whether we do anything or not," Carissa said. "When I think about that, it doesn't stress me out so much." She glanced around and spotted the issue of the *Eagle Mountain Examiner* with Jane Doe's photo on the front page. "I wonder if anyone knows who she is," she said. "She looks familiar to me, but I couldn't put a name to the face."

"Someone must know her," Danielle said. "Though it's always possible she isn't from around here. I believe the sheriff's department has sent the picture to other newspapers and television stations around the state."

"She looks a little bit like me." Carissa held the photo up alongside her own face. "If I had a sister, but I don't."

Danielle glanced from Carissa to the photo. There was a definite resemblance, though Carissa had blue eyes and blond hair, and a small scar on her chin. She had the same nose, though. "I think maybe she had a very common face," Danielle said. "That could make it difficult to identify her."

Carissa laid the paper back onto the coffee table. "Poor thing. I hope someone figures out who she is." Her phone pinged and she pulled it from her pocket and glanced from the screen. "I'd better go," she said, and heaved to her feet. "That was Joey. He worries when I'm gone too long."

"Thanks for stopping by," Danielle said as she walked to the door.

"We'll get together sometime for lunch," Carissa said. "We'll go shop for baby clothes or something." She waved goodbye and clomped down the steps, then headed up the driveway.

Danielle watched her go, a lightness in her chest that hadn't been there earlier. She had been in Eagle Mountain less than three weeks and she already had three friends here, if you counted Caleb. And surely he counted. She wasn't going to make the mistake of kissing him again, but she felt that if she needed anything, she could call on him for help, and that meant he was a friend, right?

Chapter Nine

Caleb tried to spend every other Thursday afternoon in the historical society archives, cataloging and organizing the various collections of documents and photographs the group had amassed over the years. The work required him to be both detective and time traveler and he looked forward to seeing what treasures he might unearth each week.

Most of the time he had the archives annex—a tiny space next to the historical museum that had once been used for storage—to himself, but on this Thursday he was interrupted by a visitor. "Is it okay if I come in?" Danielle asked from the open doorway.

"Of course." He moved out from behind a worktable piled with file boxes. "It's good to see you. How are you doing?"

"I'm doing well." She looked around the cluttered space—three walls lined with bookshelves filled with file boxes and a long worktable with more of the same. "I saw your truck parked outside and decided to stop by. I wondered if you ever found any information about the Silverpeak Mine that might help identify Jane Doe?"

"I haven't had much time to dig into it." He pulled a chair from the wall and positioned it nearer the table where he was working. "What kind of information do you think would be useful?"

"This really isn't my area of expertise," she said. "My job is to do the facial reconstruction, not to investigate the crime. But I have some time on my hands while I'm waiting to begin my next job and I've been curious."

"You have a new job?" He focused on clearing a space on the worktable, though his whole body was tense, waiting for her answer. "In Denver?"

"No. I've agreed to do some work for the Junction sheriff's office."

"Will you be staying here?"

"Yes." She settled into the chair. "I've agreed to rent my apartment from Butch for a while."

Relief washed over him. He stopped his busywork and smiled at her. "That's great. I'm glad."

"I think it's the right decision, for now."

He sat also. "Will you be doing another reconstruction?"

"Yes. Butch convinced me I could offer my services on a freelance basis and stay here."

"That's great."

"I hope so." She studied the bookshelves around them. "Do you have any information on the mine?"

"We have a file on the mine." He stood and scanned the shelves until he found the right box and pulled it down.

"How did you get so interested in history?" she asked.

"My dad was a history buff," he said. "On our summer vacations, we would visit old ghost towns and look for artifacts. Or he'd take me to places like Little Bighorn and talk about the battle. I thought the stories were interesting. The more you read history, the more you realize the people in the past were just like us. I always think about the kind of life I might have led in another era."

"You'd like to go back in time?" she asked.

He shook his head. "No way. I wouldn't mind visiting, but give me indoor plumbing and hot showers any day. Not to mention laws against slavery and universal suffrage and all those social reforms." He slid the box onto the table and opened it. "There's not a lot in here," he said, and pulled out a slim folder. Inside were a few black-and-white photographs and a newspaper clipping.

The photos showed a man in knee-high leather boots, canvas trousers and a patterned shirt, a neckerchief knotted at his throat, a bushy moustache obscuring his mouth. A note inscribed in ink on the back said *Silas M, Silverpeak Mine*. "Silas Malloy founded the mine in 1889," Caleb said.

A second photo was of the mine itself, with a date of 1934. "That was probably taken after the mine closed," he said, moving his chair closer to lean in beside her.

She picked up the newspaper clipping. Underneath an image of crossed pickaxes, bold black letters proclaimed:

For Sale! Silverpeak Mine 20 acre lode mining claim in the San Juan Mountains, accessible by good dirt road. 1,000 feet of well-ventilated mine tunnel. Rich mineralized quartz veins. Twelve miles from town of Eagle Mountain. Serious inquiries only.

"The ad dates from 1934, the same year as the photograph," Caleb said. He slid his laptop in front of him and began typing. "I'm checking the land records for a history of ownership.

Here we go." He moved the laptop so that it was situated between them. Danielle leaned in to study the image on screen, her head almost touching his. The scent of her shampoo, vanilla and spice, wafted to him, and he found himself focused on the soft curve of her cheek and the line of her jaw.

"I count seven different owners since 1889," she said.

Her voice pulled his attention back to the computer. "Yes. The current owners, Davis and Sarah Krupke, purchased the claim from the county last year," he said. "A number of these old claims reverted to the county when the property taxes went unpaid for several years in a row."

"Do you recognize any of the names on this list?" she asked. "Simmons, Perez, Frances, George, Aldifer, P.H. Williams trust?"

"None of them are familiar to me," he said. "I'd have to do a lot deeper digger to determine if any of them had local ties. The Krupkes told me they don't have any family in the area."

"Who else would know about that air shaft?" she asked.

"Anyone who had spent time up there hiking or maybe hunting," he said. "It's private land, but there is public land in the area, too. And since no one lives there, a lot of people don't think of exploring these old mines as trespassing. I had never been up there before Search and Rescue got the call, but I imagine there are people who grew up here who know all about the place."

She pushed the papers away. "I don't think we're going to get anywhere with this," she said. "Clearly, I'm not cut out to be an investigator. I've just started, and I'm already frustrated." She angled toward him, her knees brushing his. "Do you know if anyone has contacted the sheriff with ideas about who Jane Doe might be?"

He replaced the photos and clipping in the folder and returned them to the box. "Why don't we walk over there and ask? It's not far."

"You don't have work to do?"

"Nothing that can't wait." He would rather spend time with her. He stood and replaced the box on the shelf, then closed the laptop and slid it into a case. Case in hand, he followed her out and locked the door behind them.

The walk to the sheriff's was only two blocks, but she was out of breath before they had gone half a block. "Are you okay?" he asked, stopping to wait while she caught her breath.

She nodded. "I'm fine."

At the sheriff's office, Office Manager Adelaide

Kinkaid looked up from her desk at the back of the reception area. She regarded them from behind purple-rimmed bifocals. "What can I do for you two?" she asked.

"We're wondering if anyone has identified Jane Doe?" Caleb asked.

"You were just wondering?" Adelaide looked more severe. "I think when the sheriff is ready to share that information with the public, he will."

"We're not really the public." Caleb leaned on the desk, an easy smile crinkling the corners of his eyes. "I'm the person who brought up Jane Doe out of the mine, and Danielle is the person who gave her a face."

"And I'm sure we're all grateful to you both, but that doesn't make you entitled to privileged information," Adelaide said.

The door from the inner offices opened and Deputy Jake Gwynn stepped out. "Hey, Caleb," he called. He glanced at Danielle, then Caleb. "Is something wrong?"

"We're trying to find out if anyone has identified Jane Doe since her photo ran in the paper last week," Caleb said.

Jake shook his head. "We've had a few people call in and say she looks familiar, but we don't have a name yet. Or even anything that sounds convincing."

"I told them when we have a name, the sheriff will make an announcement," Adelaide said.

"He probably will," Jake agreed. He turned back to Caleb and Danielle. "But we don't have a name yet."

"Thanks." Caleb smiled at Adelaide. "And thank you, Ms. Kinkaid."

He and Danielle left the building. As soon as they were on the sidewalk, she burst out laughing. "Could you be any more charming?" she asked. "You were practically flirting with her."

"I obviously wasn't charming enough," he said.

She took his arm. "Charm is overrated, believe me." They walked together, back toward the history museum, where she had left her car. He liked the feel of her by his side. They couldn't be more than friends, at least right now, but that was enough.

She was panting again and he stopped, alarmed. "Are you sure you're all right?" he asked. "Do you have asthma or something?"

She stopped and put one hand on his arm and the other over her stomach. "I don't have asthma," she said. "I'm pregnant. Some pregnant women get out of breath."

He stared. He was looking at her and hearing her words, but part of him was in the living room of his old apartment in Denver, with

Nora as she made the same announcement. Only Nora hadn't said *I'm pregnant*, but *we're pregnant*.

"Are you okay?" Danielle asked.

He came back to the moment. "I'm not sure what to say."

"You can say congratulations," she said. "I'm happy about it."

"Then congratulations. Of course."

"Before you ask, yes, the father is my ex and no, he wants nothing to do with me or the baby. Which is probably for the best."

She set out walking again and he fell into step beside her, resisting the urge to take her arm once more. "Is there anything I can do to help?" he asked.

She looked amused. "You don't have to do anything," she said. "I just thought it was time I told you. It's going to be pretty obvious before much longer."

"Sorry," he said. "I guess asking if you need help is just my default mode."

Her smile made him feel as if he had stumbled off the curb, though he was standing still. "It's one of the things I like about you," she said.

They set out walking again. When they reached her car, she turned toward him. "About that kiss the other afternoon—" she began.

"You understand why I can't get involved, don't you?" he asked.

"I understand. And I'm not ready, either." She touched his arm. "But I'm glad we're friends."

"Me, too." He opened her car door and held it while she slid inside. "If I hear anything more about Silverpeak Mine or Jane Doe, I'll let you know," he said.

"And if you hear anything about Nora, let me know that, too."

"I haven't told anyone else about her," he said.

"All the more reason to talk to me about her," she said. "I'm good at keeping secrets."

He was still standing on the sidewalk in front of the history museum when Sheriff Walker approached. "Hello, Caleb," he said.

"Hello, Sheriff."

"I need you to come down to the office with me," Travis said.

What person who hears that question doesn't feel a spike of nerves? Caleb tried to quell his alarm. "Is something wrong?"

"I have a few questions for you. About Jane Doe."

Chapter Ten

Caleb sat across from Sheriff Walker and Deputy Shane Ellis in the same room where he had given his initial statement about the retrieval of Jane Doe's bones from the mine's air shaft. That had been an informal, friendly interview. Caleb had understood that he was there to fill in details for the investigative report, not as a witness to any crime. Today felt different. No one was smiling or making idle conversation. The sheriff explained the session would be recorded, then recited the Miranda warning Caleb had heard on countless television dramas.

"Am I a suspect in something?" Caleb asked, his mouth dry.

"This is just a formality," Travis said, but Caleb didn't believe him. He wondered if he should have a lawyer. Probably. But he was too anxious to know what this was all about.

"You've been asking a lot of questions about

the woman who was found at the Silverpeak Mine," Travis said. "Why is that?"

How did the sheriff know Caleb had been asking questions? He had tried to be subtle, but obviously he had failed. He forced himself not to fidget. "I'm curious," he said. "It's not every day I'm asked to retrieve an entire skeleton from an old mine shaft."

"Is it just curiosity?" Travis asked. "Do you think you know who the woman is?"

"I don't know who she is." He could say that with certainty now that he had seen Danielle's reconstruction. That face was not Nora's.

"Davis Krupke told us you've been back to Silverpeak Mine at least once since the bones were retrieved."

"I took Danielle Priest, the forensic reconstructionist, to the mine. At her request."

"You and Ms. Priest have become friends?" Travis asked.

Caleb stiffened. "What if we have?"

"You might have befriended her as a way of getting the first look at her reconstruction of the skull."

He flinched, but only inwardly, and hoped the sheriff wouldn't notice. That had been part of his motivation to get to know Danielle, but that had fallen aside long ago.

"The person who murdered Jane Doe would

have a strong reason for wanting to influence the reconstruction artist," Travis said.

"I didn't try to influence Danielle." He looked at the sheriff and the deputy's impassive faces, heart pounding. They thought he had killed that poor woman. He leaned toward them. "Look, I was worried that I knew who that woman was. Not because I killed her. But because a woman I knew in Denver has been missing for a while now. I was afraid Jane Doe might be her."

"Who was this woman in Denver?" Travis asked.

"Her name is Nora—Eleanor—Shapiro. Or Eleanor Garrison. She's my estranged wife." The last words left a bitter taste in his mouth, and he didn't miss the wary looks the two cops exchanged.

The sheriff pulled out a chair and sat across from Caleb. "Tell us about Nora."

Caleb poured out the whole sorry story, including Nora's claim that she was looking for him, and her purchase of the yellow Mustang in Paradise. "I can give you the contact information for the private investigator I hired to find her," he said when he was done. "But I believe Nora is alive and well. Jane Doe isn't her."

"Did your wife wear a wedding ring?" Travis asked.

The question caught Caleb off guard. "Uh, yeah. At least, I gave her one at our wedding. For all I know, she sold it as soon as I left town. What difference does it make?"

"Was there anything special or significant about the ring?" Travis asked. "Was it a family heirloom? Did you have it engraved?"

"No. It was just a gold band with diamonds. I bought it in a jewelry store in Las Vegas." Only later had he remembered how Nora had steered him toward the more expensive of the three rings they had been considering. She had shed tears and exclaimed that this was the ring she had always dreamed about. He had felt ten feet tall when he handed over his credit card, proud to be making her so happy.

"Do you still have a record of the purchase?" Travis's next question brought him back to the present, and the stuffy interview room. "Maybe. I charged it to my credit card. Why?"

Again, Travis and Deputy Ellis exchanged looks. "Jane Doe's ring finger on her left hand is missing," Travis said. "Her killer may have removed it if he was unable to get the ring off. He may have believed the ring could connect him to the dead woman."

"So you're saying you think Jane Doe's husband murdered her?" Caleb asked.

"It's one possibility."

"Nora is still alive. Or she was six weeks ago," he said. "I may hate her for what she did to me, but I didn't kill her."

"Do you have a photograph of your wife?" Travis asked.

The way Travis said those words—*your wife*—grated, but Caleb clenched his jaw. He pulled out his phone and scrolled to the only photo he had kept of Nora. He hadn't saved the picture to remember her by, but to show others who might have seen her. He had snapped the picture in Las Vegas, in front of the Bellagio Fountains, the day after their wedding. She struck a flirtatious pose, one hand behind her head, chin tilted, smiling with a seductive look in her blue eyes. "She doesn't look anything like Jane Doe," he said, and handed the phone to the sheriff.

Travis studied the photo. "I'm forwarding a copy for our files," he said. He did so, then returned the phone and stood. "Thank you for talking to us," he said. "Everything you've told us today will be kept confidential."

Caleb didn't say anything, just straightened and followed Deputy Ellis out to the sidewalk. When he was alone again, he stood for a moment, breathing in the spring air, heavy with the scent of daffodils from the beds in front of the sheriff's department. Had the sheriff believed him? Maybe. He had to see that Nora and Jane Doe looked nothing alike. But that solace was overshadowed by the old shame that he had let lust or greed or loneliness make such a mess of his life.

Things were getting better, he reminded himself, and set out walking back to the history museum. But they would never be right again until he found Nora and severed his ties with her for good.

THE FOLLOWING MONDAY Danielle had her first appointment with Dr. Stefanie Ambrose, her new ob-gyn. "Everything is right where it should be for your sixteenth week," Dr. Ambrose said, after she had examined Danielle. "I'm going to schedule you for an ultrasound to get a closer look but I don't expect any surprises. Are you interested in knowing the gender of the baby?"

"Yes." She wanted to know everything she could about her child.

"The nurse will give you a packet with a lot of information you'll want to know and the receptionist will set up a schedule for regular appointments. Don't hesitate to call the office if you have any questions. Someone from our birthing center will also be getting in touch with you. Do you have someone you would like with you in the birthing room? A relative or friend?" Danielle had already told the doctor that the baby's father would not be involved.

"I don't know." She didn't have a sister and her mother was dead. She couldn't imagine Butch in that role. Caleb? They were friends, but they weren't that close. "I'll think about it," she said.

"It's not a requirement. It's all about whatever you find helpful."

She left the office with a plastic bag full of paperwork to sort through, and a follow-up appointment in four weeks. Talking with the doctor had made her feel excited about welcoming her child into the world, but the checklists and appointments and growing to-do list overwhelmed her. Could she really do this?

She stashed the bag of paperwork in the back seat of her car and drove to the Mesa County Sheriff's Department. By the time she walked into the lobby there, she was back in professional mode. She identified herself at the front desk and a deputy arrived to escort her to the sheriff.

Gordon Alvarez was a tall dark-haired man with a firm handshake. "Thank you for coming all the way out here to pick this up," he said, indicating a plain white hatbox on the corner of his desk. "I have a file here with everything we know about our John Doe, which isn't much. His skull and partial skeleton were found in a field next to I-70, very near the county line. The electric co-op purchased the land last year as the site of a new solar array and uncovered the bones during construction. The details are in the folder."

Danielle lifted the lid of the box and peeked inside. A weathered brown skull lay cradled in tissue paper inside. She replaced the lid. "I should have something for you in two weeks," she said.

"That would be great," the sheriff said. "Butch speaks highly of you, and I looked at pictures of your work online. Very impressive."

"Thank you."

"Call me or the medical examiner if you have any questions. Both of our contacts are in the file." He handed over a sealed manila envelope.

Danielle arranged the hatbox and file on the back seat, next to the items from the ob-gyn. Already her mind was busy cataloging all the things she would need to do once she was in her lab. She should stop on the way home and buy some deep basins for cleaning the skull, and she might need to order some more wire to fashion armatures for the ears. She would know more on closer examination, but her first impression of the skull sutures had been of an older man, perhaps in his fifties?

She fastened the seat belt over the hatbox and made sure it was secure. She might not have any idea what to expect from pregnancy and delivery, but she was a pro at her job. It was a relief to have something to focus on that she was sure of.

CALEB WAS SITTING down to eat grilled pork chops and salad when he received a text from Sheri: Car in River, MM 16, County Road 8.

He looked at the pork chops, then back at the phone, then stood and stuck his plate in the refrigerator and went to collect his gear.

At Search and Rescue headquarters, Sheri briefed her volunteers. "According to the emergency dispatcher, the car went off the road near that big curve just past mile marker 16. The driver and a passenger managed to climb onto the roof. A driver who was following called it in." She scanned the group. "Who's completed swift water rescue training?"

Only Sheri, Tony and Ryan in tonight's group had the proper certification. "The rest of you can help out on shore," she said. "The dispatcher is sending an ambulance to the location as well."

County Road Eight wound alongside the

northern arm of Grizzly Creek before it entered the canyon, through dense stands of trees in the national forest, with an occasional pullout mainly used by fly fishermen. The white Land Rover had gone off the road at one of these pullouts and was stranded mid-river, the hood completely under the surface, water pouring in the open windows. A man and a woman were sprawled on top of the vehicle, faces white in the flashlight beams the two sheriff's deputies on scene, Jake Gwynn and Dwight Prentice, directed at them.

A stout woman in a denim jacket stood with the deputies. After Sheri had greeted the officers, she spoke up. "I'm the one who called it in," she said. "I was following those two." She jerked her head toward the couple on top of the SUV. "I already had my phone out to call 911 because their car was swerving all over the road. It looked like they were having some kind of argument. The man—he was driving—hit the woman in the head and she lunged at him. That's when the car went in the river."

Sheri set the others to work unloading gear and setting up safety lines, then she pulled out a battery-operated hailer and addressed the couple. "This is Eagle Mountain Search and Rescue," she said. "Stay where you are. We're sending people out to help you. Do what they tell you and you'll be safe."

Caleb, fellow rookie Anna Trent and Danny Irwin helped Tony, Ryan and Sheri into life jackets, helmets and safety harnesses. Carrying PFDs, helmets and harnesses for the two people on the top of the car, the trio moved into the water. Caleb waited with the others on the shore. They had donned life jackets and helmets also, in case they needed to go into the water to assist, but their primary duty was to watch and wait.

Though only a few minutes passed, it seemed much longer before Sheri, first in line, reached the car. She spoke with the people there and handed up the life jackets and helmets. The woman, a blonde in a billowy dress, was clearly frightened, and it took several minutes before her husband and the others persuaded her to go with Sheri. She screamed when she slid off the car into the water, but Sheri and Tony held her fast and began to carry her, floating her through the deeper current, then helping her across the shallower, rockier section of the river closer to shore.

Caleb and Anna swept in to take over as soon as the trio reached shore. "This is Carissa Miller," Sheri said as she unclipped the safety line from the woman's harness. "She lives in

Eagle Mountain and she's twenty-three weeks pregnant."

Caleb realized now that what he thought had been the woman's billowy dress was actually a baby bump. "Is Joey all right?" Carissa tried to turn and look toward her husband.

"Your husband will be fine." Danny moved in to take over. "Let's get you over here to the ambulance and warmed up," he said. "You're going to be fine, too."

Caleb ferried hot packs and blankets to Carissa at the ambulance before hurrying to help with the woman's husband, who had reached shore. He grabbed another blanket and more hot packs for the man, but stopped short when he saw Deputy Gwynn with him. "What happened?" Jake asked.

Joey Miller pulled off the helmet and slicked back his wet hair. "I don't know what happened," he said. "The car just went off the road into the river."

"The driver behind you called in the accident," Jake said. "She said you and your wife were arguing."

"How would she know that? She wasn't in the car with us."

Deputy Prentice moved in. "Have you had anything to drink tonight, Mr. Miller?" he asked.

"No." He turned to Caleb. "Give me one of those blankets."

Caleb obliged and turned to head back to the Beast. Jake fell into step beside him, while Dwight stayed with Mr. Miller. "Did Mrs. Miller say anything when you walked her to the ambulance?" he asked.

"No."

"I'm going to see what I can get out of her while Dwight keeps her husband away."

Instead of returning to the Beast, Caleb followed Jake, curious. Carissa Miller was sitting on the rear bumper of the ambulance, a blanket around her shoulders, another wrapped around her torso, a blood pressure cuff on her arm. "Hello, Mrs. Miller, I'm Deputy Gwynn," Jake said. "Is it okay it I ask you a few questions about what happened?"

"Uh, I guess so." Carissa looked wary.

The paramedic checked the blood pressure cuff. "You're doing great," he told Carissa, and began unwinding the cuff.

Jake moved in beside her. "What happened?" he asked. "Why did the car go off the road?"

"I don't know," she said. "One minute we were fine, the next we were in the water." She wrapped her arms around herself. "I was never so scared in my life. Is my husband all right?" She tried to look past Jake.

"Your husband is fine. The driver who was following you said it looked like you and your husband were fighting."

Carissa flushed. "Oh, it was just a silly argument. You know, the kind married people have. Joey was distracted."

"The other driver said your husband hit you."

Carissa put a hand to her cheek, then quickly dropped it. "I'm fine. Really."

"Where were you coming from this evening?" Jake asked.

"We were on our way home. Joey had taken me to see the site of a new job he was working on. He's a builder."

"What was the argument about?" Jake asked.

"It was nothing. Really." She looked up as Joey approached.

"That cop gave me a ticket for reckless driving," he said. "Can you believe it?"

Danny's arrival cut off Joey's complaint. "How's your arm and shoulder doing?" he asked Carissa.

"My arm and shoulder?" She looked confused.

"I was trying to think where I knew you from," Danny said. "Then I remembered. You were in a wreck probably two years ago, out on County Road Seven. You had a broken arm and shoulder."

"She's doing great." Joey moved closer and patted his wife's shoulder. "So great she doesn't even think about it."

Carissa smiled, though Caleb thought her eyes looked troubled. "Of course. You're right. I had forgotten about it."

The paramedic who had examined Carissa earlier returned. "How are you feeling?" he asked.

She stood. "I'm great," she said.

"You should probably call your doctor and make an appointment for him or her to check you out," the paramedic said.

"She'll be fine." Joey put his arm around her. "When we get home, she can put her feet up and rest."

"How are we going to get home?" Carissa asked.

"I called Bill back at the job site and he's coming to get us." He craned his neck and looked toward the road. "That's his truck now."

The Millers left and the ambulance followed shortly. Caleb joined the rest of the Search and Rescue crew in gathering their gear. "What was all that about an accident last year?" Caleb asked as he and Danny carried totes of PFDs to the search and rescue vehicle.

"February, two years ago," Danny said. "The vehicle—another SUV just like this one, come to think of it—hit a patch of ice and went into the trees. The sheriff's deputy told me their investigation showed the car was going way too fast when they hit the ice."

"That was the same woman?" volunteer Carrie Andrews asked. She shoved another plastic tote into the back of the Beast. "She looks different."

"She wasn't pregnant at the time, but it's the same woman," Danny said. "I remember the name. I don't know any other Carissas."

"Was the husband involved in that other accident, too?" Carrie asked.

"He was driving," Danny said. "He was wearing his seat belt, but she wasn't. She swore she had it on, but I'm the one who checked her out in the car and that seat belt wasn't fastened."

"Maybe she didn't want to admit she wasn't wearing a seat belt," Tony said. He added a tote of helmets to the gear. "She didn't want to get a ticket."

"Or maybe she was trying to get out of the car to get away from her husband," Anna said.

They all turned to look at the rookie volunteer. Anna shrugged. "If they were fighting today, maybe they were fighting then. I didn't like the way he kept answering questions for her."

"She was fine today," Sheri said. She pulled

the keys to the Beast from her pants pocket. "It's not our business to speculate on other people's lives."

They all piled into the vehicle. As Caleb fastened his safety belt, he glanced out the window and saw a wrecker backing up to the river's edge. Speculation may not be their business, but weren't they supposed to help people who needed them?

Still, Carissa Miller had been physically fine, and hadn't seemed afraid of her husband. Couples did argue sometimes, and distracted drivers had accidents. That was probably all that had happened tonight. Not everything unusual was sinister.

Chapter Eleven

The skull of John Doe absorbed most of Danielle's attention over the next few days. The man, whom she judged to be in his late fifties, showed evidence of having lived a hard life. He had worn tobacco-stained teeth, a jaw that had been broken at least once long before he died and a small round hole at the back of his skull, which had been identified in the report she had received from the sheriff as created by a small caliber bullet, the likely cause of the man's death.

She had reached the point in the reconstruction process where she was applying clay in careful layers between and over the depth markers when the pain in her lower back forced her to stop. She glanced at the clock and realized she had been working nonstop for over four hours.

She stretched to ease the tension in her muscles, then found her water bottle and drank deeply. She needed to get away from the work for a while, to breathe deeply and get her blood flowing. She would take a walk, then eat some food before she returned to John Doe.

The day was mild, with a slight breeze stirring the limbs of the evergreens that filled most of the yards she passed. At the end of the street, she stopped at Carissa's driveway. She hadn't seen her friend in a couple of weeks. Had Carissa been looking for her on her morning walks?

Danielle turned up the driveway and mounted the steps to the front door of the Miller house. She rang the bell and after a moment heard footsteps approaching on the other side of the door. Carissa opened the door, "Hey, Danielle," she said.

She was wearing a loose sundress, her dark roots grown out another half inch since Danielle had seen her last, and there were dark circles underneath her eyes. "Are you okay?" Danielle asked. "Have you been ill? Is the baby okay?"

"The baby is fine." Carissa smiled. "Come on in."

Danielle followed her through a front entry hall all the way to a sunroom at the back of the house. Carissa sank into a padded chair. "I've been meaning to call you, but I just haven't had the energy," she said.

Danielle perched on a wicker sofa across from her friend. "What is it? What's happened?"

"I'm fine, really," Carissa said. "And the baby is fine. I'm just shaken up. Joey and I were on the way home from a drive out to one of his job sites the evening before yesterday when the car went into the river. Icy water started pouring in and we had to climb onto the roof and wait for Search and Rescue."

"That must have been terrifying." Danielle imagined clinging to the top of a vehicle in the dark, surrounded by churning icy water. "But you're sure you're all right?"

"I am." Carissa nodded. "The paramedics checked me out and yesterday I went to my doctor. He says the baby and I are both fine. The experience just shook me up."

"I imagine. And Search and Rescue came and got you off the car?"

"Yes. That was the most terrifying part. I had to go into the river and they helped me through the water to shore. I learned to swim when I was a kid, but not well, and I'm really afraid of deep water. Plus, that water was ice-cold and the current was so strong. I was terrified the rescuers would lose their grip and I would be swept downstream." She rubbed her hands up and down her arms as if warding off a chill.

"Was Caleb there?" Danielle asked. "Caleb Garrison?"

"I don't know any of the names of the people who helped us," Carissa said. "Who is Caleb?"

"He's just a friend."

"Oh?" Carissa leaned toward her. "What kind of friend? Is he good-looking? How did you meet?"

"Really, he's just a friend. Butch introduced us." She was anxious to turn the conversation away from her and Caleb. "How did your car end up in the river?" she asked.

Carissa wrinkled her nose. "It was really stupid. Joey and I were arguing and he wasn't paying enough attention and drove off the road."

"I'm so sorry."

"It's okay. Joey apologized for getting so upset. His problem is, he worries too much and with the baby coming, he worries even more. He just wants to protect me and that's sweet, really."

It could be sweet, Danielle thought. Or it could be a way of controlling another person. Richard had been like that, manipulating her to do the things he wanted under the guise of concern over what was best for her. Part of her had realized what was happening even as she gave in to his *suggestions*. She hadn't wanted to make waves, to risk upsetting or even losing him. But in the process she had almost lost herself.

She didn't say any of this to Carissa. She didn't see how any good could come from meddling in a friend's marriage. "I'm glad you're all right," she said instead.

"I am. And Joey is better, too. He's just been really stressed about work lately."

"What kind of work does he do?"

"He's a contractor. He builds houses mostly, from big custom homes to off-grid cabins. He has crews, but he still does a lot of the work himself. He's good at what he does, and that allows me to stay home with the baby. Of course, it's great that you can work at home. You set your own schedule, right?"

Danielle nodded. "It is. I got a new assignment this week that I'm working on."

"Another skull, right? I went online and looked up some stuff about what you do. It's amazing, but kind of creepy, too."

"I know it is for a lot of people," Danielle said. But she didn't think of the skulls that came to her as creepy. They were part of a person, the part that held all the clues she needed to present their face to the world again and, she hoped, bring justice and comfort to their families.

Carissa put her feet up on an ottoman. "What else have you been up to?" she asked.

"I had my first appointment with my new ob-gyn."

"And how did that go?"

"She said everything looks good. I have an ultrasound tomorrow. And she sent me home with a huge stack of things to read. It's a little overwhelming."

"Don't let it get to you," Carissa said. A wall clock behind Danielle struck five o'clock and Carissa lowered her feet and sat up straighter. "Joey will be here soon and I know you probably need to get back."

"I'd like to meet Joey," Danielle said. But she stood also.

"I'm sure you will, some day. But he's so tired when he gets in from work, I like to let him really relax, you know?"

"Of course." They said goodbye and Danielle walked back to her apartment. The conversation with Carissa had unsettled her. Talk of arguments and Joey's bad moods worried her, but she had never been married herself. Maybe that was what living with another person was like.

Butch was on his front porch and Danielle walked over to join him. "How was your walk?" he asked.

"All right," she said. "I stopped in to see Carissa Miller. Apparently, she and her husband were in an accident a couple of days ago. They were arguing in the car and he was distracted and they ended up in the river."

"Is she okay?" Butch asked.

"Yes. She says they're both fine. Do you know Joey Miller?"

"I don't," Butch said. "I believe he does some kind of construction work?"

"Yes. Carissa hurried me out of the house just now because she said Joey would be home soon and he was always in a bad mood after work. It struck me as odd."

"Couples sometimes fight, and husbands are sometimes grumpy," Butch said. "So are wives. All you can do is keep listening and be ready if she asks for help."

Danielle nodded. "I'm probably just sensitive because of what happened with Richard. I don't want to be one of those people."

"One of what people?"

"The people who swear they can never trust anyone again because they were betrayed once. I know every man isn't like Richard."

"It's not the other person you have to trust, is it?" Butch said. "It's yourself."

She sighed. "I was taken in by a man before," she said. "How do I know I won't be again?"

"My crystal ball is out for repair." Butch stood. "But you're a smart person, and smart people learn from their mistakes. That means you probably won't make the same mistake again."

"I'll just make new ones."

He patted her shoulder. "That's what makes life interesting."

She sat back, one hand on her abdomen. She would never think of this child as a mistake, but because of it she had to be more careful. Now the choices she made affected two people.

"Do you know where Peach, Colorado, is?" Dan Phillips of All Points Investigations began his phone call to Caleb with this question.

"It's east of Junction," Caleb said. "Why? Is Nora there?"

"She was," Phillips said. "Last week she was staying in a motel there. She checked out three days ago and we haven't tracked her down yet. But we will."

Caleb sat, his heart pounding so hard it ached. "Why is she hanging out near me but not trying to see me?"

"Maybe she's watching you, getting a feel for your life now," Phillips said. "Or maybe this has nothing to do with you. Maybe she has another mark."

A mark. A man with a target on his back that showed he would be easy prey. Caleb had never thought of himself that way before, but Nora had seen that in him within minutes of their first meeting.

"I'm right here. I'll look for her," Caleb said.

"Not a good idea," Phillips said. "For one thing, what are you going to say to her when you see her?"

Caleb had wasted far too much time thinking about this. In the early days after her betrayal, he had composed long speeches that attempted to shame her. But people like Nora didn't feel shame, he was pretty sure. And telling her how much she had hurt him would probably only make her feel she had accomplished one of her goals. "I'll hand her the divorce papers and tell her my attorney will be in touch," he said.

"You'll have more self-control than most people if you do that," Phillips said. "I've had clients before who personally confronted their exes in cases like this and more than once the client ended up in jail. One time my guy was charged with attempted murder after he fired a gun at the woman who cleaned out his bank account."

"I don't own a gun," Caleb said.

"I still don't think you should confront her. Leave it to my employee to serve that decree. Not to mention, you're apparently on some sheriff's radar already. Someone from the Rayford County Sheriff's Department called and asked about you and Nora. What's going on?"

Caleb suppressed a groan. "I volunteer with the local Search and Rescue group," he said. "We recovered a woman's skeleton from a mine shaft. I was curious and started asking questions and I guess the sheriff thought that was suspicious. He wants to make sure the remains don't belong to my estranged wife."

"I let him know Nora was alive and well as of three days ago," Phillips said. "But do yourself a favor and stay away from Nora and avoid any trouble."

Caleb saw the sense in Phillips's plan. As much as he believed he could remain calm around Nora, he wasn't absolutely sure. She had been so skilled at knowing just what to say to sway him. What if he fell for some lie she fed him again? "All right," he said. "But there aren't that many people on this side of the state. It's not like Denver. Your employee ought to be able to find her."

"And we will. I promise."

Caleb ended the call, then paced his apartment, restless. He needed to do something, besides what he wanted, which was to get in his truck and drive straight to Peach in search of Nora. He grabbed up the phone again and punched in Danielle's number.

She answered on the second ring. "Hi, Caleb."

She sounded happy to hear from him. He relaxed a little. "Do you want to have dinner with me?" he asked. "Not a date, but I had some news about Nora and I'll go nuts if I stay in this apartment by myself tonight. And I'd love to see you."

"Of course. Come over whenever you like."

"I should take a shower," he said. "How about if I'm there about six? You can pick the restaurant."

"Sounds good. I'll see you then."

Already feeling better, Caleb ended the call and headed for his bedroom. If anyone could make him see sense about Nora, it would be Danielle. She was, he realized with a start, his best friend.

DANIELLE REMOVED THE clay-stained smock she worked in and decided the leggings and blouse she had put on this morning would have to do. She was running out of clothes that fit. She would have to take Carissa up on her offer of a shopping trip soon. She brushed her hair and freshened her makeup, then turned her attention to the apartment. Not that she had to clean for Caleb. He was her friend and he didn't care if the furniture was dusted or the dirty dishes loaded in the dishwasher. But she cared, so she did these chores, humming to herself.

When the knock sounded on the door, she glanced at the clock and saw it was only 5:30 p.m. Caleb must have decided to come over early. She hurried to the door and checked the security peephole. A teenage girl stood on the doorstep, almost obscured by the two-foot-wide arrangement of roses she carried.

Danielle pulled open the door. "Are you Danielle?" the girl asked.

"Yes."

"Then these are for you." The girl shoved the arrangement at Danielle, who took it. She stared at the collection of two dozen deep red roses, baby's breath and some kind of ferns. "Who are they from?" she asked.

"There's a card." The girl was already skipping back down the steps.

Danielle maneuvered the arrangement into the house and set it on the kitchen counter. She fumbled among the ferns and flowers and found a pink envelope and opened it.

The first thing that registered was the signature at the bottom of the page—a large and showy

Richard, the *R* written with a flourish worthy of calligraphy. With a feeling of dread, she scanned to the top of the note and began to read.

> *Please accept these roses as a small part of the apology I owe you. I let my own pain at your leaving overpower my common sense and my love for you. I made a grievous mistake in ever letting you go. I want to be a part of your life. A part of our child's life. Sometimes it takes almost losing something precious to make a man see its true value. Please forgive me and say you will be mine forever.*

A shudder ran through her and she dropped the note as if it had burned her. The paper fluttered to the counter and lay beside the flowers, writing side down. But she didn't have to see the words to remember them. They were burned into her memory. They were beautiful words. Exactly the kind of sentiments that would have made her melt before and rush back to his side.

But now she saw them as glib lies, manipulative and poisonous.

She wrapped her hands around the vase, intending to dump the arrangement in the trash, but a knock on the door made her freeze. For one heart-stopping moment, she feared it was

Richard, come to gloat and welcome her back into his arms. Then a familiar voice called. "It's me. Sorry I'm a little early."

She hurried to open the door to Caleb. "I'm so glad you're here," she said.

"What's wrong?" He took her arm and walked with her into the living room. "You're dead white and you're trembling."

"Richard sent me those. Just now." She pointed to the flowers.

Frowning, Caleb approached the arrangement. He spotted the note and picked it up and read it. "He seems to take it for granted you're going to forgive him," he said.

"Because I always did before." She folded her arms and glared at the roses as if they were responsible for ruining what had been, until they arrived, a good day.

"You don't look very forgiving just now," Caleb said. He turned toward her, his back to the flowers. "It sounds like he's trying to manipulate you."

"He is! But I'm not falling for it." She began to pace, too agitated to stand still. "But can he force me to share the baby with him?"

"Maybe you should consult a lawyer," Caleb said.

She stopped and faced him. "Yes. That's exactly what I'll do. Thank you."

"From what you've told me, it doesn't sound like this man is really interested in being a father," Caleb said. "He's saying what he thinks you want to hear."

"He is. That's what he always does."

"Nora was like that, too. It took me a long time to realize it."

She stopped her pacing. "I almost forgot. You said you had heard something about her. What is it?"

"The investigator I hired says she was in Peach, until three days ago."

"Wow. That's really close. Do you think she'll try to contact you?"

"I don't know."

"Do you want to hear from her?" She watched him carefully, but his expression didn't change.

"Yes and no," he said. "Yes, because then I would know where she was, exactly. I could give her the divorce papers and that case could proceed."

"You can't get a divorce if you don't find her?" she asked.

"I could. But it's more complicated and expensive and takes longer. I just want this to be over with."

"I wish Richard would disappear and never bother me again," she said.

Their eyes met, his full of sympathy. "We're a pair, aren't we?"

"It's a good thing we have each other," she said, then wanted to bite back the words. She and Caleb were friends. New friends, at that. There was no *each other*.

"Meow!" The cat, who retreated to her usual hiding place under the bed when Caleb arrived, had decided to come out and meet him.

"That's Mrs. Marmalade," Danielle said as the cat wound around Caleb's ankles.

"Aren't you pretty?" He stooped and ran his hand along the cat's flank. She responded with a purr Danielle could hear across the room.

"You've obviously won her over," Danielle said. Some people said animals were good judges of character. Or was it merely coincidence that Mrs. Marmalade had never liked Richard?

The cat moved on to her food dish and Caleb straightened. "Have you thought about where you'd like to go for dinner?" he asked.

"Not really." She looked again at the flowers. "Why don't we stay here? We can order in."

"Pizza?" he suggested.

"Yes."

He pulled out his phone. "Any special toppings? Peppers? Pickles? Ice cream?"

She laughed.

He gave her a mock look of innocence. "I thought pregnant women craved all that stuff."

"This pregnant woman doesn't. But get Canadian bacon for a topping instead of sausage or pepperoni. Spicy stuff doesn't agree with me right now." She had endured an uncomfortable night thanks to the barbecue they had shared after their visit to the mine.

He ordered the pizza. "What should we do while we wait?" he asked, after he had pocketed his phone once more.

"Let's get rid of these flowers," she said. "And burn that note."

He picked up the flowers and followed her onto her back balcony, where Butch had installed a small gas grill. She turned the knob, hit the striker and one of the burners flamed. Then she held the note over the flame until it caught and watched it burn to ash, which fell into the bottom of the grill.

"What about the flowers?" Caleb asked. He stood right behind her, holding the heavy arrangement in both hands.

She studied the bouquet for a moment, then plucked a single rose from the bunch. She stood at the railing and began plucking off the petals. "He loves me not," she said, and let a handful of petals flutter to the ground. She grabbed another bunch. "He loves me not."

When all the petals were gone, she threw the naked stem to the ground and reached for another rose. "You might as well get in on this, too," she said. "Otherwise, it's going to take a long time."

Caleb stood beside her and demolished roses with her. Then they did away with the baby's breath and ferns. She tossed the vase in the kitchen trash just as the pizza arrived.

They ate seated side by side on the sofa, knees touching. "Thank you for coming over," she said. "I feel so much better now."

"I invited myself over, remember?" He popped a piece of olive into his mouth. "I feel a lot better. At home I would have sat and brooded."

"Exactly," she said. "It's harder to brood when you're with someone else."

He continued to look at her, and the air in the room shifted, warmer and heavier. She was aware of his thigh pressed against hers, the masculine bulk of him, not threatening but enticing. It would be so easy to lean into him. To tilt her head up toward him and kiss him.

Easy, but not smart. She leaned forward and snatched up the remote control. "Want to watch a movie?"

They watched an action movie so bad it was funny, and took turns making fun of what was happening on the screen. By the time the movie was over and he stood to leave, she felt easy in his company again. "We'll have to do this again," she said, as she walked with him to the door.

"I'd like that." He leaned forward and kissed her, but only on the forehead. The kind of kiss exchanged between friends. It wasn't what she really wanted, but it would have to do for now.

Chapter Twelve

The text for Search and Rescue volunteers came in while Caleb was still drinking his first cup of coffee the next morning. Hiker stuck on ledge, Castle Peak. He didn't know where Castle Peak was, but a hiker on a ledge sounded like something they would need climbers for. He booted up his computer and sent a message that his 8:00 a.m. online class was canceled due to an emergency, then grabbed his Search and Rescue jacket and headed for the station.

"A passing motorist on his way to work this morning spotted this guy signaling across the valley and called it in," Sheri said to the group that gathered at the station. "We haven't been in contact with him, so we don't know the situation. Be ready for anything."

"We always are," Tony said.

They followed directions from Dispatch to the location where the reporting party had spotted the man on the ledge and Sheri trained a pair of binoculars on the face of the mountain. "I see him," she said, after a moment. "One guy, standing up, waving a piece of bright orange fabric. Good for him, having that in his pack." She passed the binoculars to Tony. "How did he get up there, and how are we going to get to him?"

"Eagle's Nest Trail is just the other side of that face," Tony said.

"My girlfriend and I were up there a couple of weeks ago," Eldon said. "There's a lot of deadfall to detour around on the middle section of the trail. We ended up turning around. Maybe this guy was trying to hike around that section and got lost."

"Back to my second question," Sheri said. "How do *we* get up there?"

She pulled out a map and they all studied it for several long minutes. "I think we're going to have to drive up to here." Tony pointed to the end of a faint line on the map that marked a four-wheel-drive road. "Then hike over to here." He took a pencil and sketched a faint line along part of the hiking trail, then cross-country toward the cliff face.

Several of the volunteers let out a groan. "Why the groans?" Grace whispered.

"We're going to have to lug a ton of equipment over that rough country with us," Hannah said. "So get ready to suffer."

The hike proved as grueling as predicted. Caleb shouldered two coils of heavy rope and a belt full of carabiners, brake bars, anchors and connectors that clanked with every step. He had more rope, an extra safety helmet and various splints and other first-aid supplies in the pack on his back. The other volunteers were similarly laden, but no one complained. They put their heads down and followed Tony, who was breaking trail over the rough terrain full of fallen beetle-killed pine trees.

"Too bad the Mountain Rescue Association observers aren't with us on this call," Danny said. "We could have enlisted them to carry some of this gear."

It took over an hour of hard hiking before they were in sight of the cliff edge. Tony began shouting, "Hello! Is someone down there?"

"Over here! Help!"

They kept calling back and forth, following the voice until it sounded as if it was directly below them. Tony lay on his stomach and looked over the edge. "Hello!" he shouted. "We're from Eagle Mountain Search and Rescue. Someone on the highway spotted your signal."

"Boy, am I glad to see you," came the answer. "I climbed down here thinking I could find the trail and now I'm stuck."

"What's your name?" Tony asked.

"Zane. Zane Nesbitt."

"Do you have any injuries, Zane?"

"No. I'm just hungry and thirsty. I've been up here all night."

"All right, Zane, we're going to come down and get you, but give us a bit. We're going to need to rig a system to do this safely."

They moved back from the cliff and huddled together to plan a strategy. "There's a sloped ramp down to the ledge he's on," Tony said. "But it's all loose gravel and scree. We're going to have to set up a rigging system to lower someone down. Then we'll have to haul Zane up."

"Caleb, are you up for the climb down?" Sheri asked.

"Absolutely."

"Great. Ryan and Tony, you're with me on the rigging. The rest of you can help with the haul up. And somebody put together food and water to send down to Zane."

Though Caleb had seen it before, he was impressed with how quickly the team fashioned a rigging system, setting anchors and stringing a spiderweb of ropes, pulleys and brake bars that would allow him to descend and he and Zane to climb back up safely.

He replaced the first-aid gear in his pack with a harness and helmet for Zane, along with an extra bottle of water and a couple of protein bars. "We're ready when you are," Ryan said.

The sun had heated the face of the cliff, so that the rock was warm beneath his palms as he started his rappel. The climb down was short, but more than once he had to rely on the rigging to catch him when the ball-bearing-like gravel of the slope slid away under him. How had Zane gotten down to that ledge without flying off into the canyon?

He touched down on the ledge next to Zane, who had plastered himself against the rock to give Caleb plenty of space. "Hi, Zane, I'm Caleb." He offered a hand to a stocky, red-bearded man in his late thirties or early forties.

"Hi." Zane shook Caleb's hand, his fingers cold. "Thanks for doing this."

"No problem." Caleb eased off his pack and took out the helmet and harness. "First, put these on. Have you ever done any climbing before?"

"No."

"Well, you're about to have your first experience." He showed Zane how to put on the harness, then clipped him to the safety line he had brought down with him. Then he handed the other man a bottle of water and the protein bars. "Enjoy your breakfast, then we'll head up."

While Zane ate, Caleb turned his back to the cliff and enjoyed the view. This was not the highest he had ever been, but close to it. He could barely make out the gray ribbon of the highway far below. A hawk soared by, almost at eye level, and the landscape spread out below like a child's school diorama.

"I don't think an energy bar ever tasted so good," Zane said.

Caleb turned back to him. "Are you ready to go up?"

Zane glanced up. "I'm ready to get out of here, and I guess this is the only way to do it."

"It is. But don't worry. You'll be safe. If you slip, the lines will catch you, and I'll be with you all the way."

The ascent was not as fast as the trip down, but almost. The tension on the ropes made it easier to walk without slipping, and once Zane figured this out, he lost all hesitation. Hands reached out to help him over the lip onto relatively flat ground, then turned to assist Caleb. While the others tended to Zane or helped dismantle the rigging, Sheri assisted Caleb. "You did a great job," she said. "Not just with the climb, but keeping Zane calm."

"Thanks," he said. "I enjoyed it, really. The climb, and working with Zane. Being part of the team effort. I've seen it all come together before, but it impresses me every time."

Once the equipment was collected, they started the hike down. Caleb stuck close to Zane, who told them about his last-minute decision to head to Eagle Mountain to hike. "I did this trail a few years ago and loved it," he said. "But this time it was different. All those downed trees confused me."

"Next time you'll let someone know where you're headed, right?" Sheri said.

"I will definitely do that," he said.

"But you did a lot of things right," Sheri said. "You kept your cool and you signaled with that bright fabric."

"It's my rain shell," he said. "My brother made fun of me when I bought one that color, but I guess it came in handy, after all." His lip trembled and he looked down. "It's just now hitting me that I could have died up there. If that motorist hadn't seen my signal. And if you guys hadn't found me…"

Caleb put his hand on Zane's back. "You didn't die. That's what's important."

Zane nodded, but was silent the rest of the hike down.

They gave Zane a ride to his car parked at

the trailhead, then rode back to headquarters. They were unloading gear when Sheri emerged from the small office, waving a sheet of paper. "Good news," she said. "We've passed the review and have been recertified with the Mountain Rescue Association for another five years."

A cheer rose from the group. "It was that rigging diagram I drew that did it," Ryan said.

"The reviewers write that they were very impressed by our team," Sheri said.

"They should be," Tony said.

Caleb should have been tired after the morning he'd had, but he felt energized. For all the things he had done wrong in his life, he needed days like this to remind him of the things he had done right. He was a good teacher and he liked to think he made a difference in his students' lives. And his work with Search and Rescue made a difference, to people like Zane and to his fellow volunteers, who could depend on him. When the situation with Nora got him down, he needed to remember that as much as she had stolen from him, she hadn't taken everything good.

The Saturday after her pizza and movie evening with Caleb, Carissa and Danielle drove to Junction to shop for maternity clothes. "I'm down to one pair of pants and a dress I don't like that still fit," Danielle said. "I have to buy some clothes."

"I don't have to buy anything, but I probably will," Carissa said.

They headed for a street lined with shops and set out to peruse the offerings. Danielle found two pairs of pants and three tops at the first place they stopped. "Don't quit now," Carissa said. "You're on a roll." She led the way to the next shop. On the sidewalk she leaned closer to Danielle and said, in a confiding tone, "You don't have to tell me if you don't want to, but you already know I'm nosy, and I have to admit I'm curious about your ex. Your baby's father? Or did you do one of those sperm donor things?" She held up a hand. "Just tell me it's none of my business and I promise I'll shut up."

Danielle laughed. "It's okay. I don't mind talking about it. He was a man I met through my work."

"You mean a cop or something?"

"He was an assistant district attorney."

"Okay, go on. Sorry I interrupted."

"He was good-looking and charming, and I thought he was *the one*." She put the words in air quotes. "And then I got pregnant and he said he couldn't be a father and I had to get rid of the baby."

"And you told him to get lost."

"Something like that. He tried to talk me into getting back together with him, but by that time I found out he was cheating on me with someone else. He had such a big ego he didn't see why I would object to sharing him with this other woman."

"Some men are such jerks," Carissa said.

"This one certainly was. So you see, a sperm donor would be better."

"Then you were smart to get away from him when you did," Carissa said.

"I don't think he sees it that way," Danielle said. They entered a shop and headed to a display marked Spring Sale. "He had the nerve to send me two dozen roses and a note begging me to take him back."

"When was this?" Carissa pulled a dress from the rack and held it up to her body.

"Two days ago."

"Did he grovel in the note?"

Danielle sighed. "He did."

"And you weren't tempted to give him another chance?"

"After what he did? No way." Just saying that made her feel stronger.

Carissa squeezed her arm. "You're going to be a great mom," she said. "A tough woman who knows how she deserves to be treated." She turned away from the sale rack. "Let's check next door. I've heard they have really cute stuff."

They were browsing a rack of clothing labeled For the Fashionable Mom-To-Be when a woman with short red hair and freckles peered around the rack. "Carissa? Carissa Miller?"

Carissa fumbled with the top she had been holding out to admire. "Oh, hi," she said. "Gosh, it's been ages, hasn't it?"

"It sure has. And look at you. When is your baby due?"

"September 17. And you?" Carissa nodded to the woman's baby bump.

"July 14. I can hardly wait. I already can't fit into anything I own, which is why I'm here." She looked Carissa up and down. "You look great. But different. Have you done something to your hair?"

"Oh, it's just the pregnancy," Carissa said. "It's made my face fuller. Or something." She turned and took hold of Danielle's arm. "It was great to see you again, but if we don't leave right this minute, we're going to be late for my friend's appointment."

Danielle allowed Carissa to rush her out of the store. "Who was that woman?" she asked when they were a safe distance away.

"I have no idea," Carissa said. "That's why I had to get out of there."

"She acted like she knew you so well."

"I know. But you know how it is—you see someone out of context and you can't remember their name for the life of you. It's so embarrassing. I'm sorry if you wanted to keep shopping there. Maybe we can go back later, after she leaves."

"That's all right," Danielle said. "I don't know that their idea of fashionable and mine is the same."

They both laughed. Carissa patted her stomach. "I don't know about you, but I'm hungry."

"I'm always hungry," Danielle said.

"Then let's have lunch. And I'll tell you about the guy I dated before I met Joey. Now he was a piece of work."

Chapter Thirteen

Caleb taught two classes a week at the Colorado State University campus in Junction. The following Wednesday he was in the student union buying coffee after his second class when he spotted a poster with photographs of Jane Doe's head and the legend Do You Know This Woman?

He paid for his coffee and moved to examine the poster more closely. It was already fading, partially obscured by advertisements for a futon for sale and someone needing a ride to Denver the next weekend. He moved these aside and read through the description at the bottom of the poster. He hadn't paid much attention to these before: *Height: approximately 5'6", Age: 24 to 27. She has had previous surgery to repair a broken arm and a broken shoulder. If you have any information about this woman's identity, please contact the Rayford County Sheriff's Department.*

A broken arm and shoulder. The same injuries Danny said Carissa Miller had suffered in her previous car accident in February two years ago. He studied the picture again. Carissa Miller even resembled Jane Doe. But of course Carissa Miller was alive and living just down the street from Danielle. This was merely one of those odd coincidences the world was full of.

He left the student union, coffee in hand and backpack on his shoulders, and headed toward the staff parking lot. He had almost reached his truck when a horn honking startled him. He looked toward the sound and spotted a car racing toward him. He scarcely had time to jump out of the way before the vehicle sped past— a yellow Mustang convertible, a woman with long blond hair behind the wheel. She lifted a hand in salute once she was past and Caleb's heart stopped beating. "Nora!" he shouted. But she had already turned onto the street and was swallowed up in traffic.

Caleb raced to his truck and fumbled with his backpack and the coffee. The coffee cup tumbled to the pavement, splashing his slacks and shoes, but he let it lay as he leaped into the driver's seat and started the engine.

He managed to back out of the parking space and get to the street without hitting anyone, one hand fumbling to fasten his seat belt as the warning alarm beeped. When the belt clicked into place, the alarm stopped and he hit the gas and sped into traffic.

At the next corner he caught a flash of yellow out of the corner of his eye and made a sharp turn, swerving to avoid hitting a bicyclist, who raised a hand in protest. He could see the Mustang now. That had to be Nora behind the wheel. She had been a reckless driver, never signaling her turns and always driving above the speed limit, as she was doing now. He pressed the gas pedal harder, and the truck surged forward.

Without warning, she turned left at the next corner. He sped out after her, right in the path of a delivery van, which screeched to a halt, horn blaring. Caleb lifted his hand in apology but kept going, the distance between him and the Mustang narrowing.

He was within one car length of her when she turned again, into a parking lot. He slammed on his brakes and headed after her, only to be cut off by another vehicle. He stood on the brakes, narrowly avoiding a collision. The other driver glared at him, then slowly eased around him and onto the street. Caleb's hands shook as he looked around, no yellow Mustang in sight.

He eased the truck into a parking spot and shut off the engine. He could have been killed in a collision—or killed someone else. All in pursuit of a woman that he really didn't need to see. What was wrong with him?

He sat for a long while before he felt calm enough to drive home. Once there, he changed clothes, grabbed his climbing gear and headed to Caspar Canyon, a gathering spot for local climbers. Climbing always cleared his head.

In the parking lot, he ran into Ryan and Eldon and they agreed to climb together. For the next two hours he tested himself on an expert cliff face, stretching to find toeholds and footholds, muscles straining, adrenaline surging when he made it to the top.

When the light grew too dim for climbing, they retired to Mo's Pub for beers and burgers. Talk turned to recent search and rescue calls. "Do either of you know Carissa Miller, the woman we pulled from the top of that SUV that landed in the creek along County Road Eight last week?" Caleb asked.

Eldon shook his head. "I sort of know her," Ryan said. "She used to work part time at Eagle Mountain Sports, but I haven't seen her in there in a while. Maybe a year or more. Why?"

"I was on campus in Junction today and I saw one of those posters for Jane Doe—the woman whose bones I pulled out of the air shaft at Silverpeak Mine. It struck me how much the picture looked like Carissa Miller."

"Maybe she has a cousin or something," Eldon said. "Though if she was missing, you'd think Carissa would have said something. Those posters are all over the county."

"It gets even weirder," Caleb said. "The poster goes on to describe the woman's height and age, and the injuries they found on her skeleton. Jane Doe had broken her left shoulder and arm at some point—just like Carissa Miller."

Eldon whistled. "That's weird. But we know Carissa isn't Jane Doe."

"We don't even know that picture is what Jane Doe really looked like," Ryan said. "I mean, I get that there's science behind this facial reconstruction stuff, but some of it's subjective, too. Maybe that woman who did the reconstruction saw Carissa and subconsciously put her features on the skull."

"Maybe," Caleb said, though he didn't believe it. Butch had raved about Danielle's expertise in facial reconstruction, and from what Caleb had seen, she took her job very seriously.

"Anything else interesting happen in Junction?" Ryan asked.

Caleb shook his head. No sense telling them about his race to catch the yellow Mustang. The less his friends knew about that part of his life, the better.

The next day he called Dan Phillips and told him about the encounter. "My investigator is already in Junction, so I'll give him this information," Phillips said. "You're sure it was Nora?"

"I'm sure," Caleb said. "I think she was waiting for me in the faculty parking lot. It's just the kind of thing she would do, taunting me, then racing away."

"You didn't go after her, did you?"

He debated lying, but why? "I couldn't catch up to her," he said.

"If you see her again, call me right away and I'll put you in touch with my investigator. You're paying us to find her—let us do the dirty work."

Right. *Dirty work.* That about summed up the whole relationship.

DANIELLE INVITED CALEB over for dinner on Thursday night. She thought they might make it a weekly tradition. Not Friday, because that was date night. But Thursday. Friends night. They could take turns ordering takeout and picking which movies to watch. He showed up at her door this Thursday with a large shopping bag.

"What's in there?" she asked.

"You'll see." Inside, he made a show of clearing off the kitchen table, then unloaded the bag while Mrs. Marmalade jumped up beside him for a better look. A jar of pickles. Another of herring. A quart of ice cream. A large bag of potato chips. A giant chocolate bar.

Danielle surveyed the offerings. "What is all this?"

"I googled things pregnant women crave," he said. "I figure now you're all set."

Laughing, she examined the various purchases. When she got to the herring, she pushed it away. "You need to take that back with you. Fish smells are my undoing right now. Even thinking about them make me a little nauseous. I have to hold my breath while I'm feeding the cat. I told Butch last week he has to clean all his fish off-site until after the baby is born. The poor man didn't even blink."

"The power of a pregnant woman," Caleb said, and slipped the jar of herring back into the shopping bag. "So, do you want to eat all of this for dinner, or have something else?"

"I already ordered Chinese." She picked up the ice cream and put it in the freezer, and carried the other items to the pantry. "Now you have to come see my John Doe," she said.

He followed her downstairs to her lab. John Doe sat under a spotlight on the worktable, a somewhat scruffy looking man with short gray hair and deep-set faded brown eyes, smile lines on either side of his mouth and a crooked chin from his long-ago broken jaw. "It's amazing how lifelike you made him," he said.

She switched off the light and they went back outside. "I'm going to take him back to Junction on Monday," she told Caleb as they climbed the stairs back up to her apartment.

"Can you take me to meet Carissa Miller sometime?" he asked.

She turned to stare at him. "Why do you want to meet Carissa?"

He looked away. "We met on a search and rescue call. I'm curious how she's doing."

"She told me she and Joey were in an accident and their car went into the water. Is that what you're talking about?"

"Yeah," he said. "It had to have been terrifying, but she and her husband walked away unharmed. At least, I hope so. I remember she was pregnant."

"She and I went shopping last Saturday and she was fine then," Danielle said. "But I'm sure she'd like to see you. I'll call after we eat and see if it's okay if we walk down there."

They made quick work of an order of sweet and sour pork and another of chicken lo mein, then Danielle called Carissa while Caleb straightened the kitchen. "I have a friend who wants to meet you," Danielle said. "Would it be okay if we walked down to your house and said hello?"

"Sure. It's Joey's poker night and I'm here all by my lonesome and I'd love to see you and your mysterious friend."

"It's all set," Danielle told Caleb.

"What did Carissa tell you about the accident?" Caleb asked, as they walked toward the Millers' house.

"She said she didn't remember any of the names of her rescuers."

"She probably wouldn't remember me. I was pretty much in the background." He took her hand to steady her on a rough patch of ground, and she didn't object when he didn't let her go. "The woman who called in the accident said Carissa and her husband were fighting. That's why he lost control of the car."

"Carissa said they had an argument," Danielle said. "She also said it was no big deal." She hunched her shoulders. "I didn't like hearing that, but I guess every couple has arguments from time to time. Richard and I certainly did. But never anything physical."

"Nora and I never argued," he said. "Maybe because we weren't together that long. Or because she was so good at telling me what I wanted to hear." He looked at her. "I would have rather had the truth, even if it hurt."

She squeezed his hand, trying to offer the comfort words couldn't convey.

Carissa met them at her front door. She wore black leggings and a T-shirt that said Tacos for Two. "Hi, Carissa, this is Caleb."

"So you're Caleb." Carissa very obviously looked him up and down, then gave Danielle a thumbs-up.

"Caleb was one of the Search and Rescue volunteers who helped when your car went in the river," Danielle said.

"I wanted to see how you're doing," he said.

"Oh, gosh, he's good-looking, heroic and thoughtful, too. Are there any more like you at home?"

"Only if you have a twin sister," he said. "Or a close cousin?"

She laughed. "No sisters and no female cousin," she said. "Which is probably why I'm so spoiled."

"Too bad," he said. "So, how are you doing?"

"We're all great," she said. "I'm healthy, baby's healthy and Joey is happy because our insurance company totaled the Land Rover, so he gets to buy a new one. You two come on in." She led them back to the sun porch, and lowered herself into her favorite chair, while Danielle and Caleb settled on the sofa. "I'm sorry I don't remember much about that night," she said. "Except that it was terrifying, and then all these angels in life vests and helmets descended and rescued us. Seriously, thank you so much. I don't know how we would have gotten out of there if all of you hadn't shown up."

"I'm glad you're doing well," Caleb said.

He continued to stare at her, but if she noticed, she didn't react. Instead she turned to Danielle. "What are you two up to? Is this your idea of a hot date?"

"No! Caleb and I are just friends."

Carissa glanced at Caleb, then leaned over to Danielle and said in a stage whisper. "Have you looked at him? I mean really looked at him? He's amazing."

"Carissa, stop it!" Danielle protested, aware that her cheeks were burning. Even Caleb looked a little pink about the ears.

"Oh, don't mind me." Carissa sat back. "My own life is so boring I try to stir up trouble with my friends. I'm sorry."

"You said Joey is playing poker?" Danielle asked.

"Yes. Every Thursday night for years and years. Before I came along, for sure. I take advantage of him being gone to eat whatever I want and watch all the movies I love but he can't stand. It works."

Caleb stood. "I don't want to keep you from your movies. I just wanted to say hello and see how you're doing."

"It was nice meeting you." Carissa struggled out of the chair and walked with them to the door. Danielle started to follow Caleb out the door but Carissa pulled her back. "I'm sorry about the teasing," she whispered. "But he is really good-looking, and he's really into you."

"He's just a friend," Danielle said.

"A friend who wants to jump your bones." She laughed. "I'm just saying!"

"I'd better go." She rushed out after Caleb. "I'm sorry if she embarrassed you," she said.

"Don't be sorry. She was really nice."

They walked down the driveway to the street. "Are you going to tell me what that was really about?" she asked.

He looked at her.

"Seriously, how often do you go out of your way to check up on people you've helped rescue?" she asked.

"Am I that transparent?" he asked.

"Yes."

"Okay. Here's the truth. But you're going to think it's a stretch."

"Try me."

"I saw one of the posters for Jane Doe and it struck me how much she looks like Carissa."

Danielle laughed. "She does. Carissa herself pointed out the resemblance right away But lots of people look alike, I think."

"Maybe that's all this is," he said. "After all, Carissa can't be Jane Doe."

"And no sister or cousins," Danielle said. They had reached her apartment and started up the stairs. "Haven't you heard that everyone has a doppelgänger?" she asked. "And I know I've had the experience of seeing someone out in public and being sure I knew them, but they turned out to be a complete stranger. Maybe we aren't all as unique as we think."

He followed her into the apartment. Smiling, she turned to look at him, but the expression faded when she saw the pain on his face. "What's wrong?" she asked.

"I saw someone I swore was Nora in Junction yesterday," he said. "I almost had a wreck, trying to follow her." He squeezed his head between his hands. "Sometimes I feel like I'm losing my mind."

"Oh, Caleb." She wrapped her arms around him and he clung to her, his head resting against hers, warm hands pressed against her back.

She smoothed her palms up and down his spine, a comforting gesture, but she couldn't help but be aware of the muscles beneath her touch, or the crush of her breasts against his chest, or the ridge of his erection against her stomach. Caleb was her friend, but he wanted her. And she wanted him.

She tilted her head to look at him, and as if in response, he leaned in to kiss her. Something broke in her at that moment and she closed her eyes and gave herself up to that kiss, letting go of everything she had been holding back so long.

He switched from kissing her mouth to trailing his lips along her jaw, all the way to her ear. "Do you want me to stop?" he asked.

"No." She pulled him against her more tightly.

"We agreed this was wrong."

"Do you really believe that?" she asked.

"I don't know what to believe." But he cupped her breast in his hand, cradling her like something precious.

"I believe I want to be with you right now," she said.

"I want that, too," he said.

"Does it matter that I'm carrying another man's child?" She blinked back the sting of tears at the words. She didn't want it to matter, but she knew that for some men it would.

"I'm technically married to another woman," he said. "Does that matter to you?"

She didn't think of him as married. Nora's

name was on a marriage license somewhere, but she wasn't his wife. "No, it doesn't matter."

He shaped his hand to her belly. "This baby is yours," he said. "That makes it precious to me. Not the man who abandoned you."

She swallowed a sob, and then he drove back the sorrow with a kiss.

She didn't know how long they stood there, kissing and caressing each other's bodies. At some point she took him by the hand and led him to her bedroom, where they undressed. He stared at her and she turned away, self-conscious, but he drew her close, her back against his chest, his hands cupping one full breast and the mound of her belly. "You are so gorgeous," he said. "And I want you so much."

She turned in his arms and they kissed until they were breathless, then he led her to the bed. "Do you want me to wear a condom?" he asked.

"Do you need to?" she asked. "Because I certainly can't get pregnant. Is there something I should know about?"

"No. After Nora left, I got tested for every sexually transmitted disease known to man. I was freaked out she'd left behind something besides bills. But I'm squeaky clean and I haven't been with anyone since." He traced a finger along her collarbone. "I haven't wanted to be with anyone. And then I met you, and it drove me wild because I knew I didn't have any right to pull you into the mess of my life."

"I've got a mess of my own," she said. "That doesn't scare you off, does it?"

He grinned. "I don't scare easy."

"And neither do I." She pulled him close once more. She didn't think she would ever get enough of the feel of his weight against her, his hands and lips on her. He had a taut, muscular body she couldn't stop running her hands over, and when he finally moved into her, she let out a long sigh of satisfaction. "That feels so good," she said.

"We're just getting started." He began to move, and she closed her eyes and let herself enjoy it all.

He took his time, drawing out their pleasure, and using his fingers and his tongue to advantage. She returned the favor, delighting at his response to her every touch. He definitely wasn't the strong silent type in bed. She had never had a lover who was so present with her. He talked as they made love, telling her what he liked and what he wanted, and he encouraged her to do the same. When she climaxed, he looked into her eyes, and they rode the wave of desire together.

AFTERWARD, SHE LAY not in his arms but facing him, one hand on his chest. "I just want to look at you," she said. "I feel so lucky to be with you now, and I never thought I'd feel that way again."

"I know." He brought her hand to his lips and kissed her knuckles. "I'm still having a hard time not thinking this is too good to be true. You might need to be patient with me."

"I can be patient," she said. "And we don't have to rush. Not anything at all."

He pulled her close again, and she lay with her head on his shoulder and drifted to sleep, her unborn child cradled between them.

LOUD BANGING PULLED her from a deep sleep. She opened her eyes to pale light through the curtains. Caleb sat up beside her and reached for his jeans on the floor beside the bed. The banging continued, and she realized it was someone knocking on the door, and shouting.

She got up also, took her robe from its hook on the closet door and followed Caleb into the next room. "Who is it?" she asked, as he looked through the security peep.

"It's Joey Miller," he said. "And he looks really upset."

Chapter Fourteen

Caleb eased open the door, just enough to look out.

"You!" Miller, a stocky blond in need of a shave, dressed in cargo shorts and an untucked oxford shirt, pointed a finger at Caleb. "You and that woman need to stay away from my house. Stay away from my wife and my property."

Danielle shoved past Caleb. She had no intention of hiding behind him. "Mr. Miller, is something wrong with Carissa?"

"You don't need to concern yourself with Carissa. She's my wife and I'll take care of her."

"If Carissa wants to see me, she can see me," Danielle said. "I'm her friend, and I'm not going to abandon her on your say-so."

"You leave her alone," he repeated.

"What prompted this temper tantrum?" Danielle asked.

Miller's face reddened. He took a step toward Danielle, but Caleb moved between them. He was six inches taller than Joey and several years younger, and considerably more muscular. Miller looked past Caleb to Danielle. "When I came home last night, Carissa was crying. She said the two of you had been down there and obviously it upset her. A woman in her condition shouldn't be upset like that."

"Carissa was fine when we left her," Danielle said. "We didn't do anything to upset her. We only said hello, stayed a few minutes to talk, then left. Caleb was one of the Search and Rescue workers who helped when your car went into the river. He wanted to see how you all were doing."

Miller frowned at Caleb. "That's all the visit was about," Caleb said. "That was a nasty scare your wife had, going in the river like that. I wanted to make sure she and the baby—and you too—were okay."

"Well, it upset her, whyever you were there." He took a step back. "I don't like people coming around when I'm not home. Carissa comes across to people as outgoing and friendly and everything, but she's actually really shy. I try to take stress off her whenever I can."

"I'm sure she appreciates that," Caleb said. "Now that we all understand each other, you'd better go." He didn't wait for an answer but took Danielle's hand and urged her to step inside with him, then shut the door behind them.

Danielle watched out the window and waited until Joey Miller had reached the street before she turned to Caleb. "There is something wrong with that man," she said. "He probably upset Carissa, not us. You saw her when we were there. She was making jokes and having fun."

"She told us he was overprotective," Caleb said.

"That is not overprotective," she said. "That is obsessive. Controlling. Definitely not right."

He went into the kitchen and she followed him. "What are you doing?"

"I'm going to make some coffee. We'll have breakfast and then we'll drive down to the Millers. If Joey's vehicle isn't parked out front, we'll go up the driveway and make sure Carissa is okay. After that, I'll drop you back here and head home. I have a class in a couple of hours."

She stared at his back. He hadn't tried to argue with her assessment of Joey Miller. He hadn't told her she was overreacting. And he hadn't suggested she stay away from her friend. Instead he had offered a sensible solution. "Carissa was right," she said, coming up behind him and wrapping her arms around his waist.

"Right about what?" He hit the start button on the coffee maker.

"You really are amazing."

He turned and kissed her. "And I'm a half-way decent cook."

"I may never let you leave."

He made a very good omelet, which she enjoyed with a cup of excellent coffee. She could have whiled away the morning with him, but she was worried about Carissa. They dressed and drove down the road in Caleb's truck. "We could walk, but if we need to get out of there quickly, the truck will be better," he said.

He cruised slowly past the Millers' driveway while Danielle studied the house. "I don't see any vehicles," she said. "When he's home, Joey's SUV is usually out front."

"Let's chance it." Caleb reversed, then turned down the driveway. He positioned the truck so that it faced out toward the street, then he and Danielle got out and walked up to the front door.

She rang the bell three times, then beat on the door. "Carissa, it's Danielle!" she shouted. "Are you okay?"

"Maybe she's not here," Caleb said.

But the door eased open. Carissa peered out. "You shouldn't be here," she said. "When I mentioned to Joey that you stopped by last night, he was furious."

"Why was he furious?" Danielle asked. "What's wrong with friends coming to visit?"

"He doesn't like people over when he's not here. He says he would never forgive himself if anything happened to me."

"We're your friends," Danielle said. "We're not going to let anything happen to you. We're certainly not going to hurt you."

"Joey has some funny ideas," she said. "It's easier just to humor him."

Danielle studied Carissa's face closely. She looked tired, but that didn't necessarily mean anything. "Are you okay?" she asked.

"I'm fine." She looked down the drive past them. "But you need to go now. And you probably shouldn't come around for a while. Give Joey a chance to calm down."

Danielle wanted to protest that what Carissa wanted mattered as much as what Joey wanted, that he had no right to cut her off from her friends. But she doubted anything she said would make a difference. "We'll go," she said. "But if you need anything—anything at all— you call or come down to the house. Any time of night or day."

Carissa reached out and patted Danielle's arm. "You're a real friend. I promise I'll stay in touch. It will be all right. You'll see."

Carissa closed the door, and Danielle and

Caleb walked back to his truck. "She seemed okay," he said when they were in the cab.

"She did. But I still feel terrible. Like I should do something more."

He started the truck. "I remember when Nora first moved in with me. A good friend pulled me aside and asked didn't I think it was a little soon. He told me later that he had a bad feeling about her from the first time they met. But I didn't want to hear anything against her. He was trying to help, but I wouldn't listen."

"I probably wouldn't have listened if anyone had tried to warn me about Richard, either," she said. "Why are we all so naive?"

"I think we expect other people to be good and honest. And most people try to live up to that, at least most of the time."

"You mean we're naive."

"Yeah, I guess we are." He pulled into her driveway and parked behind her car. "I don't think I can ever be that open and trusting anymore, but I don't want to be cynical and hard, either."

"No, I don't want that, either. Do you think there's hope for us?"

"In Search and Rescue, they teach us that people can survive terrible injuries, so we don't give up until we're sure there's nothing else we can do to save someone. I saw that first-hand recently, when we pulled a little boy from the creek who had been underwater an hour or more. I was sure he was dead, but the rescuers didn't give up on him and he lived. That was a physical injury, but maybe it applies to emotional wounds, too."

"That's a miracle," she said.

"I saw it with my own eyes," he said. "So I guess they still happen."

"Thanks for telling me," she said. She leaned across and kissed his cheek. "And don't worry. I'm not giving up."

DANIELLE WAS IN her studio that afternoon, boxing up John Doe's head to go back to the Junction sheriff's office, when the crunch of tires on the gravel of the driveway made her walk to the door of the garage-turned-workshop and look out the small pane of glass at the top. A black sedan eased into the driveway and parked behind Butch's boat. A tall man in a tailored white shirt and gray slacks got out and frowned toward the house.

Danielle's heart convulsed as she recognized Richard. Her first instinct was to stay in the studio and hide. If he knocked on the door of her apartment, she wouldn't be there to answer. If he went to the house, Butch would send him on his way. If he thought to check the garage, the door was locked and he wouldn't be able to see her in here.

Then she was ashamed of her cowardice. A few weeks away from him had definitely made her stronger. She opened the door and stepped out. "What are you doing here?" she asked.

He turned to her, all dazzling smile. "Danielle! It's so wonderful to see you."

He spread his arms wide as if to gather her close, but she took a step back. "Don't touch me," she said.

His expression transformed from elated lover to hurt little boy. "Dani, honey, you have every right to be upset with me. That's why I drove all this way—to tell you how sorry I am." He clasped his hands to his chest in a theatrical gesture. "If you want me to get down on my knees and grovel, I will. That's how much I want to make things up to you."

The idea of Richard Ernst on his knees in the gravel of the driveway, ruining his bespoke suit pants, tempted her to call his bluff, but she discarded the idea. "I don't have anything to say to you," she said. "You need to leave. Go back to Jenna."

He lowered his hands. He looked like the real Richard now. Disgruntled. "The wedding is off. She accused me of being unfaithful."

"You *were* unfaithful."

"She didn't have any proof of that. Unless you told her."

"I haven't said a word to her."

"It doesn't matter," he said. "What's important is that I'm free now. We can be together. We can be a family." He held his arms wide once more.

She wondered if he had practiced this speech in front of a mirror. It was all so perfectly choreographed. "I don't want you anymore, Richard."

She saw the shock register. The mouse had roared. But he quickly recovered. "You need me," he said. "You're not capable of raising a child on your own."

"I am and I will."

He moved more quickly than she had expected, closing the gap between them in three long strides. He had a hold on her arm and pulled her close before she could even cry out. "Don't push me," he said. "I meant what I said before. Any judge in Denver would give me custody over you when I tell him your history."

"Tell a judge anything you want," she said. "I've already spoken to a lawyer and he said you don't have a case at all. But if you're so concerned about being a father to this child, I'll be happy to sue for child support." She hadn't actually spoken to a lawyer yet, but she would, as soon as she could arrange an appointment. She tried to pull away. "Let go of me. You're hurting me."

He didn't let go, and she wondered if she could lift her knee high enough to hit him in the crotch.

"If you get in your car and leave now, you might get out of here before the sheriff's deputy shows up."

Danielle and Richard both looked to the left, where Butch stood. He held a rifle in one hand, the barrel pointed at the ground. "This gun is only loaded with bird shot," he said. "But it hurts like hell when it hits at close range like this. I don't intend to shoot you, of course, but I will if I have to and the deputy is delayed getting here."

Richard shoved her away from him and hurried back to his car. "We're not done," he called.

Danielle stayed standing up straight until Richard's car was out of sight. Only when Butch came and put his arms around her did she sag against him. "What did I ever see in such a nasty man?" she asked.

"We all make mistakes," Butch said. "Are you okay? Did he hurt you?"

She shook her head, and pushed away from him. "He scared me a little. But he didn't hurt me. Mostly, he made me angry. Angry enough to fight him. You don't know the name of a good lawyer, do you? One who can help me make sure Richard doesn't get custody of this baby?"

"I probably know someone who can help you," he said. "Ah, here's the sheriff's deputy now. Do you want to file a complaint? I'm willing to testify that he assaulted you."

She shook her head. "That's not the fight I want with him."

"Just remember, you don't have to battle him alone."

The truth of that statement brought tears to her eyes. When she had come to Eagle Mountain weeks ago, she had felt so alone. Now she had Butch on her side. And Caleb. And maybe Carissa, too. Richard didn't like to lose, but this time he had no idea what he was up against.

Deputy Shane Ellis met them in the driveway. "I had a report of a disturbance," he said.

"My former fiancé was here, upsetting me." She hugged her arms across her stomach. "We thought he was going to make trouble, but Butch persuaded him to leave."

"Are you sure everything is okay?" the deputy asked.

"Yes, I'm fine. Thank you."

"Don't hesitate to call if that changes." He

nodded goodbye and returned to his patrol vehicle.

"Do you want some company?" Butch asked. "You could come over to my place for a while."

She shook her head. "I'm fine. I have some things to do." Nothing that couldn't wait, but she wanted some time alone to process what had just happened.

Butch nodded. "Come over if you change your mind."

Inside the apartment, Mrs. Marmalade greeted Danielle with soft meows, moving in and out between her ankles. Danielle picked up the cat and rubbed her cheek against the soft fur. But Mrs. Marmalade would tolerate such familiarity only so long. She squirmed and gave a warning growl, so Danielle reluctantly put her down.

She returned to the door and checked that it was locked. She didn't think Richard would have the nerve to return, but the stout locks did make her feel safer. He had never been violent toward her, but she had never seen him as angry as he had been just now, either.

She paced, unable to settle or focus. Finally, before she could talk herself out of doing so, she picked up her phone and punched in Caleb's number.

The phone rang and rang, then clicked over

to voice mail, his deep voice speaking clearly, in businesslike tones. "I can't take your call now. Leave your name and number and a brief message and I'll return your call when I'm able."

Disappointed, she started to end the call when her phone vibrated in her hand and Caleb's number flashed on the screen. She answered quickly. "Hello."

"Danielle? I saw you were trying to call."

"I didn't mean to disturb you," she said.

"It's fine. I'm not busy. I was just getting out of the shower. What can I do for you?"

The picture that formed in her mind of him, naked and wet, was definitely distracting. For a moment she forgot why she had called. Then the memory came to her. "Richard was here," she said.

"Your ex? In Eagle Mountain?" His voice grew more urgent. "Is he there now? Do you want me to come over?"

His readiness to rush to her defense touched her. "No, it's okay. He's gone. Butch threatened him with a shotgun loaded with bird shot."

"Whoa." A chair scraped. Was he sitting down? "Tell me everything that happened."

Telling Caleb made the incident seem less frightening. Almost comical, really. Richard's shock when she turned him down. His real fear when Butch so very casually threatened him. Her own relief that he hadn't been able to sway her. "I looked at him standing there and couldn't understand why I was ever attracted to him," she said. "He was so…ridiculous. So full of himself. I can see through his lies now. I never could before, but now I know he doesn't really want to be a father. He doesn't even really want me. But he wants someone he can control. His fiancée dumped him because she discovered he was cheating on her and he acted insulted. He thought I would come running back and he could go on as he had before—juggling multiple women and never facing any consequences. He couldn't believe I turned down an opportunity like that." She laughed.

"The old saying that love is blind isn't wrong," he said. "Nora certainly took me in."

Yes, they had both been duped by lovers, but they were getting through it. "We're survivors," she said. "We're surviving our own worst mistakes."

"We are," he said. "I don't know if I believe that what doesn't kill you makes you stronger, but I hope it makes you a little smarter."

"I feel better now, talking to you," she said.

"Me, too."

They talked a while longer, about everything and nothing. When she ended the call, she felt more at ease than she had all day. She had plenty of friends, but Caleb was special. More than anyone else, he knew what she was going through. She never worried he would judge her for making a fool of herself over Richard. And he was helping her to judge herself less harshly.

Chapter Fifteen

Danielle spent all of Thursday in Junction. She delivered John Doe's head to the sheriff's department. "This is great," Sheriff Alvarez said when Danielle showed him the results. "Hopefully someone will come forward to identify the poor man. We think he could be another victim of the I-70 killer, who was operating here in the '90s. The killer has been in prison for a decade now, but we've long suspected there are other victims we haven't yet linked to him. Knowing this man's identity might help us establish a connection."

"I hope this brings some closure for a family somewhere," she said. "Let me know if I can be of any further help."

From the sheriff's office, Danielle headed to a neighborhood of old Victorian houses, shaded by mature trees, to the office of a family lawyer Butch had recommended. Allison Schaeffer had agreed to see Danielle right away. "I've dealt with cases like this before," she said. "I'm sure I can help you."

Danielle went into the meeting expecting a straightforward, unemotional meeting where Allison would tell her what to expect and what to do next. "These cases are complicated because there's so much emotion involved," Allison had said, and handed over a box of tissues. "We want what's best for you, but also what's best for your child."

Many tears and some honest conversations later, Danielle left feeling calmer. On the drive back to Eagle Mountain, she reviewed all she had learned. If Richard was serious about being a father to this baby, she had to give him a chance. But she could hold him accountable. Despite what he might think, he didn't have all the power in this transaction. He might try to use her past mental health struggles against her, but Allison had been adamant that she would challenge any accusations he made as irrelevant.

"You were very young, under a tremendous amount of stress and still grieving the loss of your parents," she said. "Any sensible person would seek help to deal with all of that. The fact that you did proves what a great advocate you'll be for yourself and your child in the future."

Her words made Danielle feel even stronger.

Maybe she would share her story with Carissa. It might encourage her friend to confide in her more, and to ask for help if she needed it.

She slowed as she turned onto her street and neared Carissa's house. Earlier, she had texted the message how are you this morning?, but she'd gotten no reply. Despite Carissa's reassurances that Joey would never hurt her, Danielle didn't trust the man. Still, Carissa was entitled to her privacy. And Danielle didn't want to drive her friend away by being too pushy.

She drove past Carissa's driveway, but had gone only half a block when she felt compelled to turn around. She would stop in briefly to say hello. If Carissa sent her away, so be it. But she had to check on her friend.

Joey's SUV wasn't parked in front of the house. Carissa kept her Toyota in the garage, so Danielle didn't know if she was home or not. Leaving her purse in the car, she walked to the front door and rang the bell. When no answer came, she leaned closer to the door and called, "Carissa! It's me, Danielle! I just came to see if you're all right."

A shuffling sound, and then a few moments later, the door opened. Danielle stared at her friend. Carissa's eye was black, and she cradled her right arm against her stomach. "I'm so glad to see you," Carissa said.

"What happened?" Danielle pushed her way inside. She wanted to hug Carissa, but was afraid of hurting her more by touching her. "Did Joey do this?"

Carissa nodded, then burst into tears; ugly, racking sobs that bent her double. "It's going to be all right," Danielle murmured, and steered her friend gently to a chair. She found tissues and poured a glass of water, pushed these toward Carissa, then sat across from her. "You don't have to talk about it if you don't want to," she said. "But I want to know if you want to tell me."

Carissa nodded and blotted her eyes, then drank some water. Then Carissa looked her in the eye. "I've been lying to you," she said. "My name isn't Carissa. It's Cathy. Cathy Rogers."

Danielle tried to let the words register. "You changed your name?" she asked. "A lot of people do that."

"I didn't change my name. Not exactly." She trailed a finger through water on the table that had dripped from the glass. "Carissa was the name of Joey's first wife. His only wife, I guess. He and I never officially married."

"Joey's first wife?" Danielle felt sure she had missed something in this conversation.

Carissa—Cathy—nodded. "They were still married when Joey and I met. We started having an affair. I know it was wrong, but he said he didn't love her, he loved me. And I thought I loved him. I did love him, but I've been so stupid." She began crying again.

Danielle waited while Cathy wept. Some appliance—the washing machine—clicked over into another cycle and somewhere farther down the street a neighbor's lawn mower whined. Sounds that ought to have been soothing in their ordinariness, yet they made the scene before her that much more unsettling.

After a while, Cathy's sobs subsided. She drank some more water. Danielle asked the question that had been pressing at the back of her throat. "What happened to Joey's first wife?"

"He told me she left him. He came home one day and she was gone. He showed me a note she had left behind, along with her wedding ring." She twisted the plain gold band on her own ring finger. When she saw Danielle watching, she held up her hand. "This is the ring. It's engraved with Joey and Carissa's names, and their wedding date. I felt bad, not having a ring of my own, but he pointed out it might look suspicious if I showed up with a new ring. And after all, we aren't really married." She looked sad.

Danielle waited for a long moment, then said, "You mentioned she left a note."

"Oh, yeah. It said she was going to Canada, where she had family. Joey said he didn't know where, that he had never met her family. He asked me to move in with him, but he said since Carissa had disappeared and he didn't know where to find her to divorce her, the easiest thing would be for me to pretend to be her. That way I could get on his company insurance and everything. He said I looked enough like her that all I had to do was dye my hair and no one would really know."

"But surely people would know," Danielle protested. "They might mistake you for her from a distance, but if they talked to you… I would know if someone else was pretending to be someone I knew well."

"That's exactly what I said to Joey. But he said Carissa didn't have any close friends. She didn't work outside the home and all of her family were in another country." She sniffed. "I found out later that she used to work at Eagle Mountain Sports, but Joey talked her into quitting that job about the time he met me."

Danielle shuddered. Why did that sound so sinister to her? "So you went along with his plan for you to impersonate the real Carissa?" she asked.

"Not at first. I mean, I was sure no one would believe I was the real Carissa. But then we went out one night, and we ran into one of Joey's poker buddies and his wife. He introduced me as Carissa and no one even blinked. They had met Carissa once before, but I guess they didn't know her well. No one here seems to have been close to her. Joey told me that proved we could get away with it." She stared down at the table again. "He wore me down. And I guess it wasn't that hard. I was working a job I hated, living in a crappy rental. I didn't have any savings, and no medical insurance." She shrugged. "All I had to do was dye my hair blond and stick pretty close to home. I had a lot of sinus trouble and my doctor had suggested surgery, so once I was on Joey's medical insurance I decided to go through with it. And somehow I let him talk me into getting my whole nose redone to look more like Carissa's."

"What about identification?" Danielle asked. "A driver's license?"

"Joey gave me the real Carissa's to use. He said she had left it behind."

"That didn't strike you as odd?"

"I know it should have, but he made it sound so reasonable. She didn't want him to be able to track her down. She was going to Canada, where she would have to get new ID. She had her passport, so she didn't need her driver's license." She buried her head in her hands. "I just wanted everything to be easy, so I went along. I can't believe I was so stupid."

"I let my ex talk me into all kinds of things," Danielle said. "Sometimes we want to be with a person so badly—and they're so good at manipulating us—that we can't see how wrong the whole situation is."

"Thanks for saying that, but I still feel stupid."

Danielle studied the woman across from her. Cathy. A completely different person than the one she thought she knew. But still a friend who needed help. Her right eye was swollen shut, a purple bruise encircling it. "Has Joey hit you before?" she asked.

"No. This was the first time. I swear. We've argued, and maybe slapped at each other a little, but nothing like this." She gingerly touched the side of her face and winced. "He's been really touchy lately, but I thought it was just because of stress at work. But yesterday I was going through a box of stuff I found in the attic. I realized it was all pictures of Joey and Carissa. I had asked him once why there weren't any photos of the two of them and he said she had taken them all with her. But I guess he had stuck them in a box in the attic. I thought it was because he didn't want to upset me, but maybe not."

She shifted in her chair and fell silent. Danielle leaned forward and touched her hand. "What about the pictures would make him so angry?" she asked.

Cathy sighed. "Like I said, the pictures were hidden, way in the back of the attic, where Joey probably thought I would never find them. And I wouldn't have, except I thought I remembered seeing some furniture up there that might work for the nursery. There's a dresser and an antique rocking chair. But as long as I was up there, I decided to look around and I found the photos." She reached into a pocket and with a trembling hand pulled out a snapshot. "I found this."

Danielle stared at the photograph that lay on the table between them, and it was as if a wintry blast suddenly chilled the room. The woman in the photo had blond hair and brown eyes. She wore a purple Colorado Rockies T-shirt, and had one eyebrow cocked in the same quizzical expression Danielle had given her reconstruction. "It's Jane Doe," she said.

Cathy wet her dry lips. "I think so. Yes. That's what Joey and I were fighting about. When he got home from work last night, I asked him about the pictures, and what really happened to Carissa. He never answered me, just hauled off and hit me. He said if I knew what was good for me, I'd never bring up that woman again."

"Was she the woman in the car accident two years ago?" Danielle asked. "The one in which she broke her collarbone and her arm?"

"Yes. When that Search and Rescue guy asked me about that, Joey really freaked out. He told me I had almost ruined everything. But it wasn't my fault. I didn't even know about that accident." She stared at the picture. "I don't think Carissa left Joey," she said. "I think he killed her and put her in that mine shaft."

"How did he know about the mine?" Danielle asked.

"He's working up at Silverpeak Mine. He's building a house for the new owners. But he would have known about the area a long time before this job. He's built other houses on those mining claims, and he's hiked all over around there." She hugged her arms around herself and began to rock back and forth. "Danielle, I'm so scared," she said.

Fear washed over Danielle like a cold wave. "Where is Joey now?" she asked.

"He's at work." She rubbed her hand up and down her injured arm. "I thought he was going to kill me last night. I think the only reason he didn't was because of the baby. It's a boy, and Joey is really excited to have a son."

"Where is he working today?" Danielle asked.

"Up at Silverpeak Mine. Where they found those bones."

"We have to get out of here." Danielle stood. "We have to get out of here now."

WHEN CALEB PULLED into his driveway Thursday and saw the yellow Mustang parked in front of his house, he wasn't even surprised. He had been waiting for this for weeks now. Maybe months. As he walked up to the house the front door opened and Nora stepped out. She was as beautiful as ever, slender, but with curves, dressed in short shorts and a low-cut tank top that showed a lot of cleavage. It was an outfit designed to attract attention. She walked right up to Caleb, threw her arms around him and kissed him on the mouth.

He became wooden, unmoving. She stepped back, lips shaped into a pout. "Aren't you happy to see me?" she asked.

He moved back, needing to put more distance between them. "How did you get into the house?"

She laughed. "I used the key, of course. I found it under a flowerpot—the same place you kept it in Denver."

She closed the gap between them once more

and slipped her arm through his, making sure to press against him. "Come on inside. We have a lot of catching up to do." She stood on tiptoe and whispered, "I put clean sheets on the bed."

He stepped away. "I don't have anything to say to you. Not after all the lies you told me."

She didn't even flinch, showing she had been prepared for this. "Oh, that was just a little misunderstanding," she said. "After I lost the baby, I fell off the deep end." She leaned against him. "I was there all alone, and you were off in England. I started feeling sorry for myself. I probably should have gone for, like, grief counseling or something. Instead, I ran away. I was just so confused." He heard the tears in her voice and knew if he looked at her, her blue eyes would be brimming, her bottom lip trembling. It would look so real, but he knew it was all faked.

He pushed her away. "I don't believe you."

She reached out for him again. "I know I hurt you. I'm so sorry. Can you ever forgive me? I want us to be together again. I know you're the only man for me."

Danielle's ex, Richard, had said the same thing in his note. "There was never any baby," Caleb said.

"There was a baby!" Wounded voice.

He looked at her then. He wanted her to see

that she couldn't sway him. "The neighbors saw you. In a bikini. There was no baby. And you moved your boyfriend in before my plane even arrived in England."

"Jack is just a friend who needed a place to stay. You can't believe those nosy neighbors. They never did like me."

He turned away and walked toward the house. She followed, but he closed and locked the door behind him. She pounded on the door. "Let me in! You have to let me in! I'm your wife!"

He went to his desk and pulled out the envelope his lawyer had prepared, then returned to the door and opened it, making sure to block any attempt she might make to enter. "Here," he said, handing her the envelope.

"What is this?" she asked, staring at her name, typed neatly on the front.

"Divorce papers."

She tried to hand the packet back to him. "You can't divorce me."

"I can and I will." He stepped back. "You need to leave now." He shut the door in her face.

She pounded on the door. Then he thought she might be kicking it. He picked up his phone, debating whether he should call the sheriff. Then he heard the Mustang roar to life. She sped out of the driveway, kicking up gravel.

He sank onto the sofa and buried his head in his hands, spent.

DANIELLE WAITED WHILE Cathy packed a few things to take with her. Danielle would drive her to the sheriff's office, where she could tell her story and, Danielle hoped, the sheriff would find some place safe for her to stay until Joey was caught.

She picked up the photograph of Carissa—the real Carissa—from the table. They would need to give this to the sheriff. The resemblance between Carissa and Cathy was uncanny. Joey Miller definitely had a type. Or had he planned all along to replace his wife, and sought out Cathy because of her resemblance?

"I'm ready." Cathy came into the room, rolling a suitcase behind her. She had changed into jeans and a tunic, and added large sunglasses that hid most of the damage to her eye. She still cradled her arm carefully.

"We'll ask the sheriff to get someone in to look at that arm," Danielle said.

"I don't think it's broken," Cathy said. "Just sprained." She looked around the room. "I think I got everything. I know where Joey keeps extra cash, so I cleaned that out while I was at it. I figure I need it more than he does."

"My car is right out here." Danielle moved toward the front door, but froze at the sound of tires on gravel.

"Joey's back!" Cathy said. She dropped the suitcase and grabbed Danielle's arm. "You have to hide. He'll be furious if he finds you here."

"He'll have seen my car by now," Danielle said. "Come on." She raced toward the back door.

The door opened just as they reached it and Joey stepped inside. He was wearing sunglasses, so Danielle couldn't see his eyes, but there was no mistaking the menace in his voice. "Didn't I tell you to stay away from my wife?" he said.

"Your wife is dead," Danielle said. "You killed her."

Behind her, Cathy gasped. Joey stepped forward. Danielle tried to move out of his way but he grabbed her by the shoulders and shook her. "You shouldn't have said that," he said. "You're in big trouble now."

"I said it because it's the truth!" She struggled, but he only held her tighter. "Why did you do it? Why make Cathy pretend to be Carissa?"

"Because death is cheaper than divorce," he said. "It would have worked too, if you hadn't come here and figured out what Carissa looked like. Then you started snooping around here. I should have gotten rid of you before you could make trouble." He shook her again, her head falling back painfully.

"Joey, no!" Cathy cried.

"Shut up!" he said. "Both of you, shut up!" He opened the door to the left of the kitchen and shoved Danielle inside. She landed hard against something metal—the washing machine. Cathy stumbled in after her and they heard the sound of a lock sliding home.

"Joey!" Cathy called. "What are you doing?"

"I'm going to get some tools. I need to work on the water heater."

"The water heater?" Cathy shot Danielle a puzzled look.

Joey made a sound like laughter. "Gas water heaters leak sometimes," he said. "Carbon monoxide. After I'm sure you're dead, I'll call the sheriff and tell him how I found your bodies. It will be a lot easier than what I had to do with Carissa. Cleaning those bones took forever, but it had to be done. This will be better. No one will suspect the grieving widower, and people will stop asking questions about Jane Doe."

"Joey! You can't do this." Cathy pounded on the door, but Joey only walked away.

Danielle joined Cathy in pushing on the door,

trying in vain to open it. "We can't get out," Cathy said, her voice rising with the same panic that clawed at Danielle's throat. "He's going to kill us. What's one more dead woman when he's already killed his wife?"

Chapter Sixteen

Caleb tried calling Danielle to tell her what had happened with Nora. She was the only person, besides the sheriff and Deputy Ellis, who knew about his ex. And Danielle was the only person who would understand. Then he remembered she had gone to Junction today, to turn in John Doe's head and to meet with a lawyer. She probably had her phone off while she was in the meeting. "Hey, this is Caleb," he said. "Call me when you get a chance."

He went to the kitchen for a glass of water, then paced, too restless to settle. Maybe he should go for a climb. It wasn't safe to climb while distracted, but that would force him to focus on what he was doing instead of Nora.

He was changing clothes when his text alert sounded.

Car off the road on Dixon Pass. All available volunteers report.

He replied that he was on his way, then headed for Search and Rescue headquarters. Here was something even better than climbing to take his mind off his own problems.

"Sheri's at a teacher in-service training so I'm filling in," Tony said to the group of volunteers who gathered around him at headquarters. "We've got a single vehicle off Dixon Pass, mile marker ninety-seven, on the downhill side at that sharp curve."

"If people take that curve too fast, they hit the gravel and lose control," Ryan said.

"We've pulled a dozen people out of that drop-off over the years." Tony said. "Only a few of them lived. No matter how many warning signs the highway department posts, people still drive too fast, and pay for it." He glanced at his phone. "The 911 operator said another driver saw the skid marks and called it in."

"It's a technical climb down there," Eldon said. "A steep drop-off with lots of loose rock."

Tony nodded. "There may be some anchors there from previous rescues, but we want to test the integrity of all of them before we use them. If we have to, we'll set new anchors." He pocketed his phone. "Let's get going."

As they crested the pass, Caleb saw the strobing lights of emergency vehicles bouncing off the red and gray walls of the canyon, which was already in deep shade despite several hours of daylight remaining. They parked behind two sheriff's department vehicles and made their way to where Sheriff Walker and Deputy Jamie Douglas stood looking into the canyon.

"You can just see the car." Jamie pointed. "That flash of yellow there. Some kind of sports car, we think."

The sheriff passed a pair of binoculars to Tony. "I spotted a Mustang logo. I think it's a convertible, though maybe the top sheared off on the way down. I don't see any movement down there."

"Someone could be down there, unconscious," Tony said. "We've seen it before." He turned and scanned the volunteers. "Caleb, are you up for this?"

Caleb stared, only dimly hearing the words.

"Caleb." Someone shook his shoulder. "What's wrong?"

Someone—Danny—led him away from the others. "What is it?" he asked. "Are you feeling faint?"

Caleb shook his head. "I'm okay," he said, the ragged edge to his voice proving him a liar. He cleared his throat and forced the words out. "I think I know who's down there," he said.

"Who is it?" Deputy Douglas and the sheriff had joined them.

He looked past the deputy, to Travis. "You remember I told you about Nora," he said.

"Your wife."

"Wife?" Half a dozen voices echoed.

"She came to see me this afternoon. I gave her the divorce papers. She was furious and upset. She raced out of my yard in a yellow Mustang convertible."

"When was this?" Travis asked.

"Less than an hour ago."

Danny clapped Caleb on the back. "Maybe she's still alive," he said.

Caleb nodded, numb.

The others set to work. He stayed back by the vehicles, refusing to look down into the canyon. He took out his phone, wanting to talk to Danielle. But there was no signal here. He put the phone away, and looked up at the rock cliffs. The highway department had closed the road to traffic while the rescue operation was going on and except for the occasional murmured voices of those gathered here, it was peaceful.

He didn't know how much time had passed before Carrie Stevens came to stand behind him. She was pale, but looked determined. Had she volunteered for this or drawn the short straw? "We just heard from Ryan and Eldon," she said. "The driver of the car is dead. A blonde. They found her purse and her driver's license is registered to Nora Garrison." She touched his arm. "I'm sorry."

Nora was dead. He waited to feel something. Anything. But Nora had stopped being a person for him. She had been a symbol of betrayal, a cartoon villain who had stolen his money and his truck and his dignity. The flesh and blood woman he had laughed with and made love with and been confused by had ceased to exist so long ago.

He shook his head. "Don't be sorry," he said. "Not for me." He couldn't mourn Nora's end. All he could feel was relief.

CALEB HADN'T WANTED to wait around to see the others bring up Nora's body, so the sheriff drove him back to Search and Rescue headquarters where he had left his truck. Caleb appreciated that Travis didn't ask any questions or try to express sympathy. "Call if I can help with anything," was all he said when he dropped Caleb off.

"I will," Caleb said. Though he hoped he wouldn't need law enforcement ever again.

He was glad the other volunteers were still at the accident scene. At some point he would try to tell them about Nora. Maybe if they knew the truth, they wouldn't think he was a callous creep for not really mourning his wife's death.

Never mind that he hadn't thought of Nora as his wife in a long time. She had been a beautiful woman, but she'd had an ugly heart.

Instead of driving home, he headed to Danielle's apartment. She should be home right now and he needed to tell her what happened. If anyone could help him sort out his emotions, she could.

He was slowing for the turn onto Danielle's street when an SUV passed him and made the turn into the Millers' driveway. He recognized Joey Miller's vehicle. Did the man think Caleb would be angered by the aggressive move?

His mood sank further when he pulled into the driveway and didn't see Danielle's car. He pulled out his phone and punched in her number, but the call went to voice mail. He didn't leave a message. She was bound to be back soon. He would wait.

But just in case she had had car trouble and gotten a ride home, he mounted the steps and knocked on her front door. He was still there when Butch emerged from his house. "Danielle isn't home," he said. "When I drove in a few minutes ago, I thought I saw her car down at the Millers'."

"Joey Miller just came home," Caleb said. "I don't like the idea of Danielle down there with him." He started down the steps.

"What's wrong with Joey Miller?" Butch asked.

"He came over last Friday morning and told us he didn't want us around his wife," Caleb said. "He was furious, though I really don't know why. I'll just walk down there and ride back with her."

"You want some company?" Butch asked.

"No, that's okay." He set out walking, worry quickening his steps. Danielle wouldn't stay around in a dangerous situation, but she would be reluctant to leave Carissa alone if she thought her friend was in danger. Caleb hoped Joey was in a mellower mood than he had been the other day.

"WE HAVE TO get out of here," Danielle said as soon as Joey was gone. If only she hadn't left her purse, with her phone inside, in the car. But she had thought she would only be inside the house a few minutes.

Cathy hugged her arms over her stomach. "How? The door is locked and there's no window."

Danielle slowly turned a complete circle, searching every corner of the small room for anything she might use as a weapon. There was a washer, a dryer, a shelf with some cleaning supplies and the gas water heater—the water heater Joey planned to rig to leak carbon monoxide to kill them. "There has to be something we can use," she said, and turned her attention to the cleaning supplies once more. She grabbed the bottle of bleach. "I could throw this in Joey's face." But the bottle felt too light. She unscrewed the cap and looked inside. "It's almost empty," she said, not hiding her disappointment.

"I keep forgetting to buy more," Cathy said.

The door rattled. "He's back," Cathy squeaked, and grabbed Danielle's arm.

Danielle pulled a bottle of liquid detergent from the shelf. It was heavy, almost full, she judged. The door to the room opened and Joey stepped inside.

Danielle swung the bottle and hit Joey in the side of the head. He staggered, but didn't go down. Instead he knocked the jug from her hand. It hit the floor hard and bounced once before rolling to rest against the wall. Then he lunged at Danielle.

She tried to dodge, but his hand wrapped around her upper arm, fingers digging in until she cried out in pain. Then he punched her in the side of the head and pulled both arms behind her back. He bound her wrists tightly, then shoved her away.

She landed hard, on her knees, pain momentarily blurring her vision.

"Joey!" Cathy shouted. She had picked up the bottle of detergent and removed the cap. She tried to splash the liquid in his face, maybe thinking she could blind him. But her aim was off and she only succeeded in dousing his shirt.

Enraged, Joey rushed her, hammer upraised. The tool made contact with Cathy's head with a sickening sound, and she fell heavily on the floor.

Danielle screamed, and didn't stop screaming as Joey moved toward her.

CALEB TURNED INTO the Millers' driveway. Danielle's car was parked close to the house, with Joey's SUV blocking her in. Caleb was studying the situation, trying to decide if he could ease the car around the big SUV when he heard a woman's scream.

He had no memory of running to the door, but suddenly he was there, battering against it, trying to break it down. More screams, and a man's gruff voice. He pulled out his phone and called 911. He gave the address. "Joey Miller is inside with two women and I hear a lot of screaming. He's threatened the women before."

He hung up while the dispatcher was still talking, hoping his report would be enough to send a deputy this way. Then he charged the door again, pain shuddering through him at the impact.

But the door gave way, with a satisfying *craack*!

The front room was empty, but sounds of a scuffle drew him to the back of the house. A door off the kitchen stood open and Joey was just inside, struggling with someone, her screams like jagged claws tearing at Caleb. "Hey!" Caleb shouted.

Joey turned, a hammer in his hand. He didn't hesitate but charged at Caleb, hammer swinging. A lightning bolt of pain shot through Caleb's right shoulder, and he sank to his knees. Joey loomed over him again. One thought pierced through the pain—if that hammer came down again, Caleb was dead. With a groan, he lunged forward, and wrapped his arms around Joey's legs, dragging him down.

The two men grappled. Joey kicked and Caleb clawed. He couldn't hear the screaming anymore. The throb of his own pulse and his tortured breathing filled his ears over a steady stream of cursing from the man he struggled with. Another glancing blow struck Caleb on the back. Enraged, he got hold of Joey's wrist and bent it back. With a howl, Joey let go of the hammer, and Caleb threw him onto his back and straddled him. He slammed the other man's head into the floor, watching in satisfaction as Joey's eyes rolled back.

Then someone was pulling him off Joey. "We'll take care of him now," Travis said.

Caleb staggered back. Deputy Douglas steadied him. "You're bleeding," she said. "An ambulance is on the way. Why don't you sit down over here."

"Danielle," he said. "And Carissa." He looked around and spotted the door where he had first seen Joey. He pulled away from the deputy and made his way to the door. Jake Gwynn was there, kneeling over two women.

"They're alive," he said, in answer to Caleb's unspoken question.

"Caleb?" Danielle struggled to sit. Her cheek was swelling and her dress was torn.

Caleb dropped to his knees beside her and unfastened her wrists, then gathered her close. Neither of them said anything for a long time. They just held each other, not needing words.

"Can you tell us what happened, Ms. Priest?" The voice belonged to Travis, who stood over them.

"Cathy?" Danielle looked toward the other woman, who lay very still on the floor.

"She's alive," Jake said. "Unconscious, but breathing."

"The paramedics just pulled in," Travis said.

The paramedics bustled in just then. Caleb recognized Hannah Richards, the medical officer for Eagle Mountain Search and Rescue. She and her partner knelt beside Carissa Miller and began to examine her.

Travis squatted down so he was eye level with Danielle. "Anything you can tell us now would be helpful," he said.

"Joey Miller killed Jane Doe," she said. "Her name is Carissa Miller. The real Carissa Miller."

Caleb looked at the woman being tended by the paramedics. "If Jane Doe is Carissa Miller, who is that?"

"Her name is Cathy Rogers. She was Joey Miller's girlfriend." Danielle sighed. "It's a long incredible story."

"You can fill us in later," Travis said. "What happened here this afternoon?"

"Cathy didn't know Joey had killed Carissa," Danielle said. "She thought Carissa had left him and this was a way for her and Joey to be together when he didn't know where Carissa was to divorce her. She looked a lot like Carissa, and Carissa apparently didn't work outside the home and she didn't have any family or close friends in the area. Joey persuaded Cathy to dye her hair and get a nose job so she could slip into that role. But yesterday she found some photographs of the real Carissa, and she realized why Joey had been acting so stressed out since those photos of Jane Doe went public. She confronted him and he beat her up. I stopped by to see her and she told me everything. We decided to take what she knew to the sheriff and ask for his protection. But before we could leave, Joey came home."

She pushed her hair out of her face. "Could I please have some water?"

Deputy Douglas brought the water. Danielle drank and watched while they loaded Carissa/Cathy onto a stretcher. "At first, Joey locked the two of us in this room." She looked around at the small space that contained a washer, dryer and gas water heater. "He said he was going to do something to the water heater to create a carbon monoxide leak. He'd come back later and *discover* us and everyone would think we died in a terrible accident. We tried to fight him, but he hit Cathy with the hammer and knocked her out, then came after me. I kept kicking at him and rolling out of the way and screaming."

"I heard the screams," Caleb said.

"Thank God you did," she said.

Hannah knelt beside her. "That's quite a bruise you have on your cheek," she said.

"Can you hold this ice pack against it?" Danielle pressed the ice pack to her cheek.

"Do you hurt anywhere else?" Hannah asked.

"I'm a little bruised up, but I'm fine."

"Let's see if you can stand up." She helped Danielle to her feet. "How's that?"

"I'm good." She looked toward the door. "Is Cathy going to be all right?"

"I hope so," Hannah said. "She was starting to regain consciousness when we loaded her into the ambulance. That's a good sign." She slipped a blood pressure cuff onto Danielle's arm. "Let me just check a few more things."

The ambulance's siren blared, then receded as they drove away. Hannah examined Danielle, who insisted she was feeling fine. "I don't see anything to be concerned about," Hannah said. "But you should probably contact your doctor and see if she wants you to come in, just to be safe."

"I will."

Hannah turned to Caleb. "There's another ambulance on the way for you. You need to have that head injury looked at. You could have a concussion."

He opened his mouth to protest that he was okay, but thought better of it. "I need to talk to Danielle for a little bit," he said instead.

"You've got until the ambulance arrives," Hannah said.

Caleb rejoined Danielle, who was speaking with the sheriff. "We'll need you to come to the station and give us a complete statement," Travis said. "That can wait until tomorrow, but is there anything else we need to know right now?"

"You should have this." Danielle reached into her pocket and took out a photograph.

Caleb leaned in to look at the image of a smiling blond woman in a purple T-shirt. "That's Jane Doe," he said.

"It's Carissa Miller," Danielle said. She handed the picture to Travis. "You should be able to match her dental records with Jane Doe's teeth. And Carissa was in a car accident two years ago. She broke her arm and her collarbone and had surgery to repair both."

Travis slipped the photo into an envelope and then into his pocket. "We'll be in touch," he said. "Anything else?"

Danielle hesitated, then said, "Cathy is wearing a wedding ring that belonged to Carissa. Joey told Cathy that Carissa left the ring behind, along with a note saying she was going to Canada to live with family there." She glanced at Caleb. "Jane Doe's ring finger is missing. I think maybe Joey tried to get the ring off and it wouldn't budge, so he chopped off the finger. Cathy says the ring is engraved, so it would be evidence against him if he had left it with the body."

"We'll take a look at the ring," Travis said.

The sheriff said goodbye and Caleb put his arm around Danielle. "How are you feeling?" he asked.

"I'll probably be sore tomorrow." She slipped her arm around his waist. "But I'm so grateful to be alive." She studied him, eyes full of concern. "How are you doing? Joey hit you pretty hard."

He touched the tender spot at the side of his head and winced at the pain, then winced again when he saw the sticky blood on his fingertips. "I'm going to the hospital in a little bit to be checked out. But it's just a precaution. I'm sure I'll be okay. I hate to leave you."

"I'll be okay." She hugged him close. "We'll both be okay."

He kissed the top of her head. He had a feeling it would take a while before the impact of everything that had happened today hit him—a woman he once loved was dead, and the woman he loved now had narrowly escaped death.

She squeezed his hand. "I hope you were having a good day until you came to see me."

"Not exactly."

She frowned. "What happened?"

"Nora is dead."

She searched his face. "How do you feel about that?"

"Honestly? Relief. I've been waiting for the other shoe to drop for so long. Now I'm sure she can't do any more damage. But I'm sorry things ended the way they did."

"How did she die?"

He looked around them. Sheriff's deputies moved in and out of the house, some in uniform, others in white coveralls and booties. No sign yet of the ambulance. He spotted a sofa on the other side of the room. "Come here," he said, and led Danielle to it. They settled in next to each other and he told her about Nora's visit. "I've been dreading seeing her again because part of me was afraid she would lure me right back into her web. But today I found out I was finally immune to her charms. I wouldn't have believed anything she said. I handed her the divorce papers and shut the door in her face, and I felt like I was finally free."

"How did she react?" Danielle asked.

"She was furious, but she couldn't do anything about it. She tore out of my driveway in that yellow Mustang. She was always a reckless driver and I imagine she was taking out some of her frustration on the road. She missed a sharp curve up on Dixon Pass and went over. Search and Rescue got the call. As soon as I saw the car, I realized what had happened. It shook me up, but at least I know now the whole ordeal with her is finally over."

She leaned her head on his shoulder and he held her, comforted by her presence. Maybe he could get things right with her. Maybe Nora hadn't ruined him for every relationship.

"I talked to a lawyer in Junction today," she said. "She told me Richard has rights as a father, but they're not more important than my rights. If he really wants to be a part of this baby's life, he can be, but I can ask for the terms I think are safe. And we can insist on a custody trial here, where I live, and where Richard doesn't know all the judges. I felt better after talking with her."

"That's good," he said.

She turned to face him. "I think there's a good chance Richard will continue to make trouble. I won't blame you if you don't want any part of that."

"I want a part of anything you're a part of." He took her hands. "I want to be with you. You and your baby. After what happened with Nora, I was sure I didn't have any chance of future happiness. You've proved that's just another lie of hers I believed."

"I'm still nervous about diving into anything too quickly," she said.

"You don't have to dive," he said. "We'll wade out slowly. I promise to hold your hand all the way."

"And I promise to hold your hand." She kissed him, and it felt like a gift, giving back a part of himself he thought he had lost.

Epilogue

Four and a half months later

"Just a little bit more. You're doing great. She's almost here." Danielle panted and pushed as Caleb gripped her hand and provided a running soothing commentary in her ear. The pain and pressure were almost unbearable, and then a shift, cries of celebration from the birthing team around her and, a few seconds later, a loud wail. And then she was cradling her daughter, tears of joy running down her face unchecked.

"She's beautiful," Caleb whispered, and she saw the tears above his mask.

"You have a beautiful daughter," Dr. Ambrose said.

"You did it," Caleb said.

"We did it," Danielle said, and smiled down at her beautiful child.

The rest of the day passed in a weary blur. Someone cleaned her up. Someone else helped her nurse the baby. Caleb left and she slept. When she woke, he was there, cradling the baby and gazing at her with such an adoring look it brought tears to Danielle's eyes. "Hey," she said.

"Hey." He stood and transferred the baby to her. "We've been getting to know each other."

"Knock, knock. Can I come in?"

She turned as Cathy swept into the room, her own baby, Oliver, in a sling on her chest. "How are you all doing?" she asked. She leaned over for a closer look at the baby. "She's beautiful! Are you finally going to tell me her name?" It had been an ongoing debate between the friends. Danielle had refused to reveal her chosen name to anyone. Even Caleb didn't know.

"It's Lily," she said, smiling down at the infant. "After my mother."

Cathy perched on the side of the bed. "Hello, Lily," she said. "You and Oliver here are going to be great friends. Like me and your mom."

Danielle patted her friend's arm. Cathy had recovered from the physical trauma Joey had inflicted, and was in counseling to deal with the emotional side of it. She and Danielle actually saw counselors in the same building, and joked about carpooling to therapy sessions, though that had never happened.

Joey was in jail, awaiting trial for first-degree murder of his wife, Carissa Miller, and kidnapping and attempted murder of Cathy and Danielle. Cathy had bravely volunteered to testify against him, but because she and Joey were never legally married, she had lost everything. With help from friends and the state's victims' fund, she had found a job and an apartment, and was doing well.

"I brought you a little something," she said, and shifted to dig into the diaper bag on her shoulder. "Not exactly a baby present, but sort of." She handed over a folded newspaper.

Danielle shifted the baby to one arm and unfolded the newspaper on the bed in front of her. The top headline in that morning's edition of the *Denver Post* declared *Assistant DA Resigns After Accusations of Sexual Harassment*.

"Speaking out made a difference," Cathy said.

"It wasn't just me. There were five others." One of those women had contacted Danielle two months ago and asked if she would join in their complaint against Richard. "I heard you were dating him, and then you left your job suddenly and actually moved away," the woman, Felicia, had said. "I thought it might have had something to do with Richard's behavior."

Danielle had been afraid, but after talking

with her therapist, she had decided she was strong enough now to do it. Caleb had traveled to Denver with her to give her deposition, where she had met the other women, all of whom had been victims of Richard's particular brand of manipulative charm. "I'm glad he didn't get away with what he did," she said.

"Have you heard from him at all?" Cathy asked.

She shook her head. After his visit to Eagle Mountain that one time, he had never contacted her again. She had heard from the other women involved in the complaint against him that he had begun wooing another attorney in the office. That ill-fated pursuit had led to his downfall. Apparently he had finally met a woman who recognized him for what he was right away. Dealing with her had taken away any desire Richard had had to be involved with Danielle or their child.

"Another worthless man taken out of circulation, we can hope," Cathy said. She leaned over and patted Caleb's hand. "And thank you for constantly reminding me that there are good guys out there." She turned back to Danielle. "What's next on the agenda, Mama?"

"Want to help plan a wedding?"

Cathy squealed. "You're going to do it? Really?"

Danielle smiled at Caleb. "I think we're both ready."

He nodded. "And we have a little girl to raise."

"Caleb is going to adopt Lily," Danielle said. "I already told my lawyer to send the papers to Richard. I don't think he's going to put up a fight."

Cathy clapped her hands together. "And they lived happily ever after."

"Real life is better than fairy tales," Danielle said. "We're always going to have problems, but I think we're strong enough to deal with them. Together."

* * * * *

*If you missed the previous books
in Cindi Myers's
Eagle Mountain: Critical Response
miniseries, look for:*

Deception at Dixon Pass
Pursuit at Panther Point
Killer on Kestrel Trail

*Available now wherever Harlequin Intrigue
books are sold!*